Maggie and Minotaur

Maggie & Minotaur

Olwyn Harris

Reading Stones Publishing

Unless otherwise stated Scriptures quoted here are from the King James Version (Authorised version). First published in 1611. Quoted from the KJV Classic Reference Bible, copyright 1983 by the Zondervan Corporation.

Stock images from StoryBlocks.
Cloud drawing no. 3 Minotaur. Image used with permission. Original photo by Fotologic and published at https://www.flickr.com/photos/fotologic/3754021517/ Altered by Wendy Wood.

Published by: Reading Stones Publishing
                     Helen Brown and Wendy Wood
Cover Design: Wendy Wood

For more copies contact Helen Brown at:

Glenburnie Homestead
212 Glenburnie Road
ROB ROY NSW 2360
Mobile: 0422 577 663
Email: hbrown19561@gmail.com

To my beautiful daughters, Rebekah and Kathryn... and Thalia, who has joined our family so seamlessly. You are endless sources of inspiration of the strong, intelligent and independent women I admire. May God continue to bless the work of your hands and your heart...

1.

Maggie unfolded herself from the sulky. She pushed open the gate and breathed the morning air deeply, drinking in every sight and sound and smell. Everything she remembered; everything she had fantasized about; everything she had forgotten, came rushing in and it felt heady. The potato vine climbed over the lattice near the back door, its white flowers studding the green foliage like a child's painting. Lonnie's herb garden under the tank stand left a lingering twang of fresh mint and oregano in the air. Zinnias, colourful and bold, stood like cardboard cut-outs in the tubs beside the path.

She wiped her boots on the coir mat and Blinko stirred, arching his back in a morning stretch. Maggie dumped her carpetbag unceremoniously on the step and reached out to pick him up. She laughed at the rumble in his throat and shook her head, amazed that the little black and white kitten she pulled from a box on her ninth birthday could now be so fat and pampered in his retirement. "Lonnie's been looking after you well Blinko," she murmured into his ear. "My first love…" she chuckled as she juggled the latch and called into the depths of the kitchen. "Lonnie?"

Then she was there, her squat little mother, with more creases around her Asian eyes than she remembered. Her wide face broke into a grin as she shuffled to the door.

"Lonnie! Oh my…" Maggie's voice crackled momentarily as she was enveloped in her generous arms.

"Baby girl… what in God's name? It's like seeing one raised from the dead! Sammy? Sammy!" She called over her shoulder as her Sammy came through the door. He was as tall and skinny, as she was short and stout. The community never quite reconciled to Sammy for having hooked up with a Chink. It was one of those anomalies Maggie had grown up with. To her, this couple didn't seem odd. They were family.

Then the interrogations started just as she expected. Had she been well? Why was she here? What happened to the gentleman with the big house? Did she leave her aunt in good health? Why didn't she write ahead? She was so skinny… didn't Missy know how to cook? All those years with the best of teachers, how could she still look like a convict? So many questions. Maggie sat at the table and tried not to smile too broadly as she looked around at the pumpkin on the bench, the eggs in the basket, and blackened kettle on the stove. This was homecoming time; a celebration. And she gave no definite answers.

"Lonnie, I'm dying here! I would absolutely love some potato-cakes and pot of tea... your special herbal one. I haven't had real tea since... forever!"

Sammy poked around the stove and added wood to the firebox. "Tea coming up."

Lonnie looked at her keenly. "You, Missy are hiding secrets. And it is your old *Lou Mou*, you should be telling them too." She pushed back the chair, grabbed a potato from the vegetable rack and started grating it into a bowl.

Maggie laughed. "That took exactly two minutes and thirty-five seconds! Life is back to normal. Oh, you are good for me Lonnie. I have missed you so!" She bounced up and gave her a hug from behind.

Lonnie grunted and peeled an onion, grating it into the mix with an exaggerated sniffle. "Normal? Don't know the meaning of the word. Nothing is normal anymore. Sammy put the pan on the stove."

"Haven't you served breakfast yet?" Sammy shook his head and Lonnie grunted louder. Maggie retrieved the tray from its possie in the pantry and set it on the table.

"Breakfast? It is more like supper, the time they have it. Can't get into the day well, when they're sipping and nibbling and carrying on to midday." She continued her reflections in Mandarin, her disgust transparent.

"Midday?" Maggie laughed trying to picture the Landowner and his wife dillydallying on the upstairs verandah so late. That was the paramount form of depravity. Things had truly slipped at Henderson's Gap. This was getting more interesting by the moment.

Sammy silently poured a cup of tea for Maggie and sat one for his wife on the bench beside the stove. Then he added some leaves to the small teapot on the tray. Lonnie grunted and spooned mixture into the pan, tapping the side as she waited to flip the hash over. Bacon sizzled as she added some eggs and cut off a couple of slices of bread with more grunting and huffing.

Maggie smiled affectionately and put her cup back on the saucer. If she hadn't grown up with this lady she might have been concerned. Whatever was eating her would come out sooner rather than later. "Uncle Sammy, Lonnie has trained you perfectly. No one does tea like this."

Lonnie grunted again and banged the side of the pan with the egg-flip. This time even Sammy put down his cup and looked at his wife with a raised eyebrow. He said nothing but stood to his feet and took the plate over to her as she plonked the hash-brown, bacon, eggs and bread on the plate. They fell obediently into place. Lonnie picked up the tray and stomped off to deliver its contents. Sammy followed with a cloth over his arm and a jug of freshwater.

Maggie jumped up. "I understand! I get it! I'm sorry for not writing ahead." She trailed them through the house, but instead of going upstairs, they went straight to the library. "But I didn't have time really. It was all just very sudden." Lonnie grunted in response. "There is no point trying to cover it up. I know you are pleased I'm here!" Maggie said playfully giving her a hug. Lonnie stiffened as Sammy knocked on the heavy panelled door. "I knew it! Your delight at having me home is driving you crazy!" Lonnie grunted. Maggie bent down and gave her a squeeze around her middle, underneath the breakfast tray. "You, old softy," she whispered affectionately. "*Lou Mou*, you are just marshmallow underneath all this efficiency and good cooking. You are glad I've come."

The heavy door swung open. Lonnie's step forward caught Maggie off balance and she slid to her knees hanging onto Lonnie's apron. The breakfast tray went flying and the teapot shattered into a scolding pile of china, hash-browns and eggs.

Maggie looked amazed at the disaster smeared all over the polished floor in the middle of the library, a mischievous grin playing on her lips. The foremen stood at the door; his eyes openly amused. "Welcome back to Henderson's Gap Miss Maggie," he said.

She glanced up in relief. "Jones – good morning! Would you like some breakfast? There seems plenty to spread around." Her humour faded abruptly as her eyes met the startled, grim look of the man behind the desk in the middle of the room.

He stood, his hard boots hitting the polished floor forcefully. "I will eat in the Dining Room. Sammy, bring me tea and toast there. I don't have time to waste like this."

Lonnie shuffled across to allow him to pass, as Maggie was still on her knees at her feet. Jones stood with his hand motionless on the doorknob. Sammy left to retrieve fresh tea and toast.

Maggie burst out laughing and Lonnie grunted. "That, Missy, is the Captain. The Henderson's have left. He's manager now. This is our new normal."

⊰•⊱

The New Normal was nothing like Old Normal. Maggie went for a walk to allow Lonnie some space to calm down. Even scrubbing the dining room floor hardly made a dint in the volume of her huffing and puffing. It seemed Maggie always had a way of creating havoc in the respectable calmness of Lonnie's life. It was that way when she was a kid. It seemed to be her gift. She attributed most of it to poor cultural translation. Sammy would shake his head and say with affection, "The Chinese have Emperors and Empresses... and then they have Lonnie. They all get their own way without having to explain themselves."

She smiled again at the horrified look on the manager's face and Jones standing there, just taking it in. Things change, but some things don't. Maggie noticed the wear of bush-life and the sun showing around Jones' eyes, but he still had that nothing-can-ruffle-me way. He seemed very much the same. He was strong, good looking and pure as gold. He was the stockman who taught her to ride and shoot. She had spent hours sitting on the stockyard rails, watching him tackle run-away steers. He'd pick himself up out of the dust without a word. He would turn and give Maggie a wink and a grin. "Just steer'n 'em straight." It sort of became their private joke: Jones steering the steers. He did the same for jackaroos; he'd steer them straight too. Maggie never considered the disparity in their ages anything to blink at. He had been her forever hero, and even at twelve, she was going to marry him... until he fell in love with another woman.

When Maggie left for the train-station that year, gripping the side of the sulky as it rattled its way over the gutters in the track, for the life of her, she couldn't believe Jones' soon-to-be-bride could possibly be good enough for him. Maggie had refused to meet her. The whole idea that Jones had found another love was enough to send her away to school without revolt. It just couldn't be. Maggie stepped around some tall clumping grass on the track and smiled about her childish infatuation. A wife and six kids later, it hardly seemed like the twelve-year-old dream of happiness ever after. But then, some things do change. She was changed.

Aunt Winifred had seen to that. Aunt Winifred took her guardianship of Maggie very seriously: private school for her sister's only child; music and art tuition; charity events and the most elite social groups. The only blight on Maggie's years at school was homesickness, so she threw herself into everything with a driving energy that earned her a name for being competitive and zealous. She excelled in rowing and equestrian events and topped her classes academically. The perfect student, the best friend, the prettiest dancer: Maggie had the world at her feet. And the world had a name. He was tall – taller than Jones… and he lived on Fairfield Estate.

Maggie came to a rocky outcrop and sat down. Home. After all this time, she was home. She gratefully allowed herself the liberty of a quiet tear, private compensation for all those tearless years. Tearless for fear she would be seen as ungrateful and a burden. Suddenly she was twelve again and this time she privately vowed she would never leave unless she was forcibly removed. Even Lonnie's displeasure felt homely and real. Real. Yes, that is what she missed.

She sat for a while just thinking about what was real. Romance for instance… that was not real. For Maggie, the mythical Minotaur represented Romance – half man, half beast. The Minotaur was a monster created from centuries of classical Greek mythology and no normal man could withstand its strength. The only one who rose to meet this challenge was Theseus: the legendary prince. Theseus was willing to negotiate the impenetrable labyrinth and sacrifice his life to put an end to the evil perpetrated by this monster Minotaur, and he prevailed in the face of unthinkable odds.

She wondered if she was waiting for her hero, her Theseus, just like the legend. She frowned a little and contemplated what sort of injury she may have done herself by desiring this imaginary larger-than-life hero. How many real people would this illusion devour, because, unlike Theseus, they could not stand up against a monster as violent as Romance? She knew this hero was a self-creation, but really, live flesh and blood seemed so disappointing. And she also knew, if she let it, this thing could devour her, just like the mythical fate of those virgins who were sent down the labyrinth to appease the wrath of the Greek god.

She shook her head. Never mind. At the moment she was content to co-exist with this Minotaur. Seeing Jones standing in the library with that ironic twist on his lips as she clung to Lonnie's ankles was enough evidence for now. She was not ready for Fairfield Estate. Let the monster live. Let it flourish for a while. Sooner or later she would accept that Theseus, the hero, did not exist. She knew that she would have to battle through the maze of reality and confront it herself. The danger was appealing. Yes, she was sure, one day she would challenge this monster and free herself from its tyranny. That day the Romance Monster would die. But not just yet. Fairfield Estate was still too close. There had to remain a better reason to give it up and stay away.

As she sat, she became aware of a peewee's pipe-whistle chiming. She smiled and listened to the duet. The common magpie-lark's ability to play the same tune in triplets and syncopated timing with their mate was a wonder to her; each with their part; each with their unique timing. She had always thought its sound, although it was hardly melodious, was comforting in its familiarity, and a flawless picture of harmony between lovers. Somehow Fairfield Estate could never fit easily into a common peewee's companion song. It was music Aunt Winifred would never understand, because it didn't encompass the pianoforte classics. That is why Maggie made no attempt to explain why she left. She just left. She closed her eyes and took a breath. Lonnie's deep-set brown eyes would only smoulder hotter if she tarried long. She rose to go. As she did, her line of vision locked into another set of brown eyes, mischievous and wide, half-hidden behind a scrubby bush.

"Hey there..." she said softly.

"Hey there yourself."

"What's your name young man?" she enquired.

"What's yours?" he responded as his wiry frame emerged from hiding.

"Well, my name is Margaret Jane Louise Wick."

"Miss Margaret?" He giggled.

"But you may call me Maggie. My friends call me Maggie."

"Oh." He paused, eyeing her sceptically. "Well s'pose you can call me Tom then."

"Tom. I am pleased to meet you." And she nodded her head in a curtsy as he stood up tall, reaching into his pockets, slouching in a relaxed soon-to-be-man way. His brown eyes matched his muddy brown shorts, brown skin and matted brown hair.

"If you're Miss Maggie, Dad says you used to be a ripper on a horse." He looked her up and down disdainfully. "I don't believe him."

She acknowledged the backhanded compliment with a nod of her head. "Sometimes things are not what they seem." Being twelve was a life-time ago. Yet someone remembered her. Blondie perhaps. He was a jackaroo who was as black as she was fair. She just remembered him as one of Jones' steers, one of those he helped steer straight. They spent a lot of time together. "And your Dad's name would be...?"

The boy stood up tall and squared his shoulders. "Marshall Thomas Jones."

"You're Marshall Jones' kid?" Maggie sat straight up. "Jones?" So, there was more to Jones than she thought. He had a wife and six kids; Sammie confirmed that. Fancy Jones, with all his religious talk, having an aboriginal mistress and goodness knows how many bastard kids as well... like the little brown sprite standing cheekily before her.

The kid looked at her shrewdly. He was probably about seven or eight, maybe more. His wiry limbs tensed, ready to run. "Only if you're his friend. Not everyone calls him Jones." That was a matter of fact.

"Well, I believe I am your father's friend since he calls me Maggie."

She smiled to herself: Maggie and Minotaur.

2.

So here she was. Back home. One romance shattered on the rocks even before it was launched into the main current. Maggie spent a lot of time riding. Taking the back tracks away from prying eyes, feeling the freedom of the saddle under her thighs, without the restriction of a side-saddle equestrian routine. Or she would walk, and then sit closeted under callistemon trees watching swayed branches sweep the surface of the still, silent river. There was no music... no music at all. The silence was deafening. A pervading listlessness surrounded her week after week. Even Lonnie had given up asking why she had come home so abruptly.

It was Tom she bumped into on these excursions, poking his perky little head around the corner, just watching her. She came to expect he would pop up when she wasn't expecting him. She sat down and opened her book, unobtrusively trying to spot where he was. "You can come out now Tom," she said eventually. Maybe she was mistaken. Maybe he hadn't followed her today. She thought he had.

His curly head emerged. "You're getting good Miss Maggie; I'm not scaring you now."

"Oh, I don't know Tom... you are like a mirage. Sometimes I think you are there, and you aren't. Sometimes I think you are not there... and look, here you are."

He grinned and sat down beside her. She pulled a muffin from her pinafore pocket and offered it to him. He polished it off and licked the crumbs from his fingers.

"Blondie says I got the tribe in me. I am a good hunter because I am like a shadow."

"Shadow?"

"Yeah, I can disappear."

"But I can see you now."

"Only 'cause I want you to. See that bird over there? You see him 'cause he wants you to. He's not afraid."

"I don't see any bird." Maggie strained her eyes against the brown and grey-green of the scrubby bank of tea-trees, as the call of a peewee answered her challenge. She smiled and gave a soft laugh. "Tom you are very clever..." She turned to congratulate him on illustrating his point so well. "Tom?" He was nowhere to be seen.

She chuckled and stood to her feet and closed her unread book. "Shadow."

She kept shaking her head on her way back to the homestead. "Now you see me, now you don't." It was a game she wished *she* excelled at. It would be convenient to disappear any time you wanted. Just now she was grateful she had space to at least walk away. It was a luxury she had not had since she was twelve.

As she wiped her boots on the boot-jack, Blinko came and rubbed against her legs. She paused to scratch under his chin. His steam-train purr sounded so comforting. Maggie pulled off her boots before going inside the kitchen. She went to the stove and checked the kettle. The water was still hot from afternoon tea, so she helped herself to a small pot of tea. She sat at the table quietly savouring the herbal flavours.

Lonnie bustled into the room, her long skirts rustling impatiently. "Oh Missy, you are back. The Captain is asking to see you. You must come now. Hurry. You must go. He is not a man to be kept waiting. Goodness knows we do a lot of waiting on him though."

Maggie looked up; her eyebrows raised and quietly took another sip from her teacup. "But this is your job Lonnie; waiting on Henderson people." She smiled slightly amused over the brim of her cup. She was not one to jump just because someone said jump. Not straight away at least.

"Henderson's, yes. This man is not Henderson. Not a Henderson bone in his body."

"But Henderson put him on. It's exactly the same thing."

"Not even remotely the same thing, young Missy. Now put down your cup and go and see what he is wanting you for."

"I will see him shortly... after I finish my cup of tea. He can't be waiting since he had no expectation of when I would be back."

Lonnie found Maggie's stubborn lack of curiosity most disconcerting. "But Missy, he has never asked for a private audience before. This is most unusual."

"Oh!" she gasped slightly, a teasing look in her eyes. "Do you think he knows?"

Lonnie looked mortified. "Knows? Are you sick child? Is that it? Is that why you have come home? Have you got The Consumption?"

Maggie gave a small pathetic cough and then burst into laughter. "Oh goodness, Lonnie! If I had any sort of illness, serious or otherwise, you of all people would be the first to notice. I'm perfectly well!"

Worry creased further around her eyes. "Not funny. I did say to Sammy, 'That girl is very thin!' I did say to Sammy..."

Maggie interrupted her. "I'm not *thin* Lonnie: it's called 'fashionably slender'. And I haven't coughed once since I've been here. I'm teasing Lonnie – seriously. I am all right. Although I am thinking I will stay a little longer. I need to work out what I'm going to do next. I've decided I won't be going back to Aunt

Winifred's. I've written to her and asked for my things to be sent here."

Maggie quickly pushed away her teacup before Lonnie could react to her announcement, and she walked down the hall to the library.

She knocked on the door and waited for a response. She presented her empty arms as she walked through the door, "No breakfast tray Sir, out of respect for the safety of your staff. There is absolutely no danger of a scalding with eggs and bacon today."

He looked up from the desk where he sat and considered her announcement. Maggie noticed again the grim line of his mouth. Eventually, he nodded and told her to sit. He went back to his notes.

Maggie sat, uncomfortably aware of the odd situation she found herself in. Eventually, she stood up. "Sir, Lonnie said you wanted to see me. If this time is not convenient..."

He docked his pen in its holder and cleared his throat. "I have a request. I would like you to tutor my son. He is of the age where a nursery governess is advantageous. You can start on Monday. Nine o'clock. I will see Thelma has him ready each morning."

She looked at him, waiting for more... well, more details. None came. Evidently, he had said everything he had intended to say. Maggie stood still, unwilling to be dismissed. "Sir, what is his name... your son?"

He looked up; shocked she was still there.

She cleared her throat. "You have given me very little information on which I am to base a decision… regarding your *request*. What is his name?"

"Whether his name is Herbert or George, it is of no importance. He will learn just as well. Since you have accommodation here with your family, this could be considered a way of recognizing we are not a charitable institution. Nursery. Nine o'clock. That is all."

Maggie bristled. "Just tell me his name and how old he is!"

He looked at her impatiently, a dismissive flick of his wrist restrained at the last moment. "Alexander is five."

"I will meet Alexander tomorrow. Whether I take the governess position on Monday as you so generously offer, will depend on how we get along. If I do, I will be paid thirty pounds a year and of course, that will include my board and lodging. As you can see, you are not the only non-charitable folk in this room. Good morning sir," she said and gave a decisive nod as she left.

Maggie went straight back to the kitchen and Lonnie poured a cup of tea as she walked in the door, pushing it wordlessly toward her. "Despicable man," she said under her breath as she took her cup. Her hand trembled slightly as she sipped. She replaced the cup on the saucer and laughed mirthlessly. "I don't even know *his* name."

Lonnie hovered in a haze of worry. "He was a ranking officer in the Queen's army," she said as if this explained everything. "He's just *Captain* to everyone here."

3.

Maggie eyed the listless boredom in the boy's eyes as he sat in the living room. So, this was the child who belonged to the "Captain". She had seen him with Thelma, but there was nothing particular to indicate he was a child of position. A little quiet perhaps... a little sooky; but he just seemed like a kid. The thought gave her a measure of courage.

She sat down beside him. Today his light sandy hair was slicked down in a formal part to one side. She thought it looked ridiculous on a child so young. "Good morning Alexander, how are you?" She spoke softly.

He dragged himself to his feet and stared at her wide-eyed. He glanced over at Thelma who hovered around the boy like a bee with a honey pot. He shrugged and waited. He had no expectation this interview would change his life forever.

"Has your father explained he would like us to spend some time together today?" There was no reaction. She carefully watched the blank wall between them. "So..." she pushed on. "I was thinking we would go... outside." There. Just barely, there was a vague hint of interest, hardly perceivable. "Thelma, please get Alexander's walking boots; we are going for a walk."

Thelma's eyes widened, the black of her pupils larger than saucers. "Oh Miss, I don't think this is a very good idea. Not at all. The Captain is very clear about activities that may endanger the child."

Maggie saw the faint glimmer of curiosity in his eyes doused in a familiar chorus of caution. "Come, we are not going to jump off a cliff! Besides, constitutional walking is regarded as beneficial exercise by many; something I'm sure the Captain appreciates." She turned to the boy. "Now Alexander: boots on, hat on, let's go and find our adventure. There must be something exciting waiting for us today." When Thelma fussed and made preparations to follow, Maggie smiled as they paused at the door. "Thelma you work such long hours, why don't you take this afternoon to treat yourself to a pampering. Have a nice long bath... read a book... or whatever takes your fancy. Alexander and I will be fine."

He dragged his feet, and Maggie dragged his little hand. She wanted to get him out and away, to find a space where she could see if she would want to do this every day for the rest of the year... or the next... and the next. She knew outside marriage to the handsome resident of Fairfield Estate she would be obliged to find a position of sorts. Options were limited really, and here a position found her: at home.

"How old are you Alexander?"

He held up his chubby hand mutely.

"Do you like living at Henderson's Gap?"

He shrugged. He didn't indicate one way or the other.

"So, your father was a soldier. Would you like to be a solider one day? Or perhaps you prefer farming?"

She looked at him curiously. He stared blankly ahead. How could she take the position if there was absolutely no connection between governess and student? Did she have a choice? Did she have to take the job just because it was offered? Or demanded? It certainly irked her, the man's presumption and the slurs he made about charity. She didn't feel without options… yet. That was something her family's resourcefulness had instilled into her. No one can make you do what you don't want to do. Although it was acknowledged that sometimes it is expedient to change your "want to".

Did she really want to? What *did* she want? What was the music in her heart that would make it seem worthwhile?

She wanted to stay at Henderson's Gap. The space cleared her head.

She did want to stay near Lonnie and Sammy. There was something emotionally incomplete which she needed to explore after being away for so long.

She was certain of one thing: going to Aunt Winifred's had been about attending school. Now that that was over, to come home was right. Where was she going from here? How could she find direction? She allowed herself the possibility that it may take some time to work out.

She wondered if she could she ever make this sad little boy smile? There. That was it. The trump card sat on the table. She wanted to see him smile.

She picked up a river-stone from the gravel used to level the path. It was smooth and flat. A good skipper. "Alexander, do you know how to skip rocks?" He looked at her sceptically. "It is a very hard thing to do but I'm sure we could do it if we tried. Let's go down to the river to practice."

He shrugged. The mystery of physics, which causes a rock to skim on water, was not something he was the slightest bit interested in; but a little healthy competition, even for a five-year-old, was not beyond him.

"There might not be good skipping stones down on the river bank, so we need to find them before we get there. What do you think about this?" Maggie held up a lumpy rock. She pulled a very dubious, unconvinced expression. He considered her face and then shook his head. She held up another... it was flatter but still rough and uneven. He shook his head again. She shrugged. "See, together we are better at picking the right sort."

She reached down and picked up a smooth, flat stone. "I remember Sammy telling me this was a good shape. Can you feel how smooth it is? Perhaps you can see another one?" Using the stone as a template, Maggie pulled off her straw bonnet and together they heaped in likely skippers. She praised and scrutinized as the pile became bigger.

"You know, Alexander... I think we are ready to release this assortment of rock-skippers over the water." They positioned the pile close to the river's edge, where the bank was grassy and low, free from the border of reeds that clumped further along the bank. Maggie rolled up her sleeves and flexed her fingers. Alexander didn't need to know she used to be the district champion. Just now she wanted to help him find a smile in exploring the world. After some consultation, it was decided Maggie would go first. She calculated at least three skips would create the marvel of rocks dancing on water. Three skips. No more. It sunk softly under the surface. Maggie applauded and Alexander's eyes opened wide. He had no idea rocks did anything other than sink. The extent of his experience with water was the bathtub and water troughs around the homestead.

Maggie selected another and held it in his soft hand. With a flick of her wrist, it flew across the surface... four skips... and it disappeared in concentric circles with a splash. Cheers! A quiet grin spontaneously responded to her clapping. It was her sign. Delightedly she selected another, like the smooth stone David used to conquer a giant. It skimmed and danced lightly over the surface. Ripples circled around in a pirouette as it disappeared. They danced together for a long time, checking the smoothness of the performers, the number of skips, the length of the turns. For this moment the river was their stage and they had front row seats to the most spectacular show before them.

Finally, the last stone disappeared and the curtain was drawn. Maggie sat down with a contented sigh, and she reached over and took Alexander's hand. "Your father would like me to spend time with you every day. There are lots of things to learn and I would like to help you do that." She looked at him.

He looked back at her wide-eyed. "Can we come here tomorrow?"

"Sometimes we will go outside, but sometimes we won't. But always there will be something for us to do."

He shrugged, a little disappointed. He considered thoughtfully. "Okay."

Maggie let out her breath slowly. Fair enough then. She was in. She would accept the position. "Well, I can tell your father the good news. I will see you on Monday, shall I? How about nine o'clock?" He nodded as she put her bonnet back on over her dark curls.

⊱•⊰

4.

Maggie was setting some drawing things on the table and talked happily with Alexander, building anticipation about what they were going to do today. She smiled, thinking gratefully about the time she spent in the Fairfield nursery with the governess of the Hasting's twins. The governess became her very good friend and she would go there to hide whenever she wanted to escape. She helped prepare lessons and compile the resources they needed for each session. She noticed it became her habit to spend more time upstairs having fun than in the drawing room with respectable company.

He exploded into the nursery. "Unbelievable!" he roared. "Five minutes with my son and you were setting to drown him? What on earth possessed you to take such liberties?"

Maggie stepped back completely unprepared for the assault. Yesterday afternoon she had gone to the library to accept the position; he had only nodded and made a trite comment that meant nothing. She knew, of course, he assumed she'd comply with his wishes from the beginning. Maggie looked at the raw anger in his eyes and spoke very quietly to Thelma who came in behind him and stood by the window. "Thelma, please take Alexander down to the kitchen. Lonnie has prepared some morning tea for him. Alexander's father obviously has something he wishes to discuss… in private."

Thelma had a "told you so look" in her eye as she hurriedly bundled Alex out the door. Maggie held the back of a chair, her hands clammy. "You have some concern's Sir, regarding my care of your son?"

The quietly paced tone of her voice momentarily gave him pause. He lowered his voice and met her with cold aloofness. "What were you thinking to take a five-year-old child down to the river? It was blatantly irresponsible. Such an action has absolutely no relevance to his education."

"Firstly, we had not started "his education". You may recall my position as governess commenced about ten minutes ago. I merely needed to find a place where I could determine whether there would be a connection between us. If it had been evident that was not the case I would have declined the position. As it is, we had a lovely morning and I felt comfortable that…"

"What hogwash! Connection? Comfortable? Whether he likes you or not is completely immaterial! The boy is a child. I want a governess to educate my son – and that is all. A river adventure is not going to educate him."

Maggie laughed softly, a mirthless sort of chuckle. She had never thought a soldier could be so melodramatic. "Adventure? Seriously? Your son is bored out of his mind! Believe me, it took some convincing him it was possible to have an interesting morning, learning or otherwise. I'm glad we chose to go outside – we had a great time."

"He goes outside with Thelma. Just focus on teaching him to read and do his numbers. That is all that is required of you.

"Hardly enough! Learning is more than a ledger and an alphabet. Our little 'adventure' for your information covered preliminary counting, geometry and physics, biology and geology, texture and science, as well as the physical demands of dexterity and coordination. His education was well catered for in every regard! *Gratis* mind you, because I still had not *accepted* your offer. And I might emphasize, his safety was *never* compromised."

"You are never to go to the river again. You are forbidden. If you cannot comply, you are dismissed."

"Dismissed?" Maggie sat down on the chair. "None of what I have said means anything to you? I am just dismissed?" This was not exactly what she had expected.

"What I said was...*if* you do it again, you are dismissed. I am a fair man; perhaps you have not understood my expectations. But there can be no doubt now."

"So, this afternoon I am dismissed?"

"What? No of course not..." He looked at her puzzled and then, as her meaning dawned on him his rage began to build again. "You could not possibly intend to take him back there! My goodness, what sort of irresponsible ogre are you?"

"An honest one. Alexander pleaded with me. I said if we completed the activities, I had planned we would go for a walk. That is all. But I did give him my word."

"You have no right to promise such a thing! You are forbidden. You are not going."

Maggie sighed and stood to her feet and met his gaze directly. "Look, Sir, I am sorry you feel this way. I considered deeply about accepting this position and I felt it really was something that would work... for both of us. But this is not the case if you cannot trust me. You gave me no rules to work within when you offered this proposal. You didn't even seem terribly interested apart from getting a "yes" from me. Now you put me in hobbles and expect me to work with my hands tied behind my back. You won't have to dismiss me this afternoon after our excursion to the river, because as it stands I cannot possibly pursue this position. Consider my resignation effective immediately. I would, however, like to inform Alexander of this decision myself."

Maggie turned away and started packing up the things she had placed out on the table. He stared at her stunned. "Decision? How can you resign?"

"Easily it seems. Sir... you said yourself you were going to dismiss me. I'll save you the trouble and the anxiety. Find someone else to… never mind. But, can I suggest... just tell them what they are in for before you explode? I think it would be fair. For me, I have..."

"Okay, okay. You are obviously used to getting your own way. However, he is *my* son, and he is *my* responsibility."

"Of course, you are his father, but you cannot possibly be everywhere at once. If I were to be in charge of Alexander's education, I see it as doing that on your behalf. As such, I have to be able to make decisions regarding activities during that time. Nothing more. But nothing less either."

He hesitated. This was something unfamiliar for him. "Perhaps there is still a way this can work... *for both of us...* as you said."

Maggie stared at him thoughtfully. Can people really be this arrogant? "When I said I thought this would work for *both* of us, I was referring to Alexander and myself. He is the pupil, after all, Sir. As for your concerns about charity: I would request leave to remain with my relatives a short time longer. I will do my utmost to find another position as soon as I can.

You have my word — although it seems that means little to you."

He stared at her absolutely floored. Then spun on his heel and left the room. She heard him ride out on a horse a few minutes later. A lone tear escaped her lashes, and Maggie carefully wiped it back into her hairline around her temple with the heel of her hand.

She really had felt something stir inside her last night, as she lay awake, planning her day of activities. Creativity had bubbled up inside her that she found absolutely intoxicating. She could not remember anything in a very long time that had stirred her so. It was exciting... and now the dream lay smashed at the feet of an arrogant man who really was as unreasonable as Lonnie suggested. Perhaps she should not have been so dogmatic; maybe she should have tried to be a little flexible. But she knew if she couldn't be herself, she would suffocate inside. It felt like Fairfield Estate all over again. She might as well spend her energy emptying night pans from under the beds.

She sighed and picked up a slate board and drew a sad face. So much for assumptions; she supposed she was as guilty as him. She assumed this would be the start of a very satisfying relationship with a sandy-haired, blue-eyed boy with a killer smile. She rubbed it out with her cuff, unperturbed by the smudges it left and drew an angry face. He didn't try to change her mind. Nothing seemed more acceptable than getting rid of her. Well, It can't be much simpler than that. Done.

❧ • ☙

Maggie left Alexander crying with Thelma and picked up her bonnet. She had to get out. Away... down by the river. Maybe she would fall in and be swept away in its evil, manic, unpredictable torrent. She found the whole thing absurd. She was a rower. She could read its surface like a good novel. Sure, there was mystery; sure, there was a level of risk – that was some of the appeal. But mostly she found it serene. Blast to anyone who would steal this experience away from what she had to share. She picked up a couple of good skippers and put them in her pocket.

She sat down on the grass that had been witness to so many smiles the other day. She sat thoughtfully watching the surface of the water ripple under the caress of a breeze. Now. What now? It felt like a rug had been pulled out from underneath her and she had fallen hard. She didn't know how, in such a short time, she could become so committed to something, which hadn't even been part of her life before. What had changed? Nothing... and everything. It seemed all the questions she had asked, remained.

She still wanted to stay at Henderson's Gap. The space did clear her head. But now she had to acknowledge she would have to find another head-clearing space where she could hear the music of her heart.

She still wanted to stay near Lonnie and Sammy. Well, she would have to find another way. This time she would write.

She still wanted clarity on the direction she was going to take from here, and yet, in the same moment, she knew what it would be.

Yes, she still wanted to make little people smile. It just could not be that particular little boy. She had broken his heart and made him cry. But why not others? Similar, but not the same. Perhaps that was the point of this very pointless morning. Purpose out of pain. She had heard Jones say that once. She had thought it had sounded so noble at the time. Just now there was only a limited sense of nobility registering in her belly and a significant amount of gut-wrenching grief. But in that warm burning, she identified some of the energy she felt last night. She could seek another position. Why not? Someone, somewhere, would give her leave to teach the way she wanted to.

A shadow passed before her eyes and she jolted to her feet. "Hey, Miss Maggie... you were not watching for Shadows today." He danced away laughing.

"Shadow... "She looked at his cheeky smile and laughed out loud, conceding his extraordinary skill. Here was a boy who was prepared and willing to laugh.

"Tom Jones, you are just way too clever for me." She automatically reached in her pocket for a muffin, and then hesitated. "Sorry – no muffin today." She felt the smooth stones under her fingers. "I only have these..." She pulled out the stones and opened her palms. "Choose one Shadow and let's see if you can skip rocks like your Dad." He grabbed one and she stood tall. "Rules: one stone; one throw; most skips wins."

"I go first because I'm the youngest."

"Uh-uh young man. Ladies first..."

Shadow hesitated and then bowed in mischievous respect. "No matter – I'm still going to win. I'll just know by how many."

Maggie pulled up her sleeves and flexed her hands. It was a ritual that would not leave her. She flicked the stone over the surface and counted the skips with confidence.... "...five, six...." Fair – certainly not the best throw she'd ever made.

Tom maneuvered into position. "Shadow wins..." he predicted. He made his throw and jumped up and down coaxing the rock to skip further: "...six, seven-eight-nine! I win; I win!"

Maggie curtsied and shook his hand solemnly. "Sir, I yield most humbly to your victory. That was an excellent stone-skipping performance!"

He leaned over and whispered. "I would like my prize now."

Maggie raised her brow with a smile and looked around. She picked up a piece of gnarled river driftwood. She presented the award with great ceremony declaring it to be a perpetual trophy for all future stone-skipping competitions at Henderson's Gap. Tom laughed and hopped around corroboree style, waving his trophy in his victory dance, Maggie clapping her congratulations in rhythm.

❧•☙

Duncan McCray sat on his chestnut stallion and watched. He wondered how long Maggie would sit there silently, a motionless sculpture. What happened that morning when she came bursting into his life, upsetting his equilibrium with her smile and her chaos? Even Lonnie – calm, unflappable, sullen Lonnie had been different since she arrived. Nothing was the same and every protective instinct was fighting for the safety of the routines he had built around his world.

The governess thing was a bad idea, catastrophic from the start. He should have realized from the hash-browns smeared on the library floor she was not the governess for his son. What had possessed him to suggest it? Was it just the convenience of not having to advertise or go through an agency? Perhaps he had hoped her energy would bring a spark into Alexander's eyes. And he had seen it, but he now realized it wasn't a governess that lit that light, but a wild excursion. He kicked himself that his dreamy naivety allowed him to think things could be different. He sat silently astride his stead, like a European market-square statue. It suited him to feel strong, immovable, impenetrable. It was for the best, her going away. It might be awkward, unsettling, even callous; but it was for the best.

What surprised him was her insistence of going against his obvious wishes. Why should he feel so displaced? After all, he had won. He had done the same thing a million times without flinching. Why should her cool defence of her irresponsible actions be different? Perhaps because he *had* got his way, he *had* won, and no matter how many times he affirmed that to himself, it honestly felt like he had lost... something. Yet as he watched her, it seemed like she was the one grieving a loss as she sat quietly watching the reflections on the water. Still, *she* resigned. Her choice. Perhaps it was just because she had held herself so confidently and made her case so decisively and heartlessly. Okay, maybe not *heartlessly*. That was not an accurate description of what he saw. He fought in his mind to find a word to express more exactly what it was that puzzled him. Perhaps it was not heart-less, but heart-felt; or... heart-full. He had always been able to insist and enforce by disconnecting his heart. The military had taught him that. It seemed she had effectively insisted and enforced by connecting into her heart, her passion. He saw fire there, deep down. And it puzzled him. Exceedingly.

Oh yes. It had been a bad idea. And yes. It was for the best.

Resolved that he had now settled the situation in his mind, he turned in the saddle to go when he saw the Jones' kid sidle up beside her. She had been lost in thought, and it was an irony to him that he was not the only one in deep contemplation after this morning's encounter. Possibly he had not expected deep thought or clever articulation from one who laughed so readily. He guardedly watched as she started to her feet, wondering what impudence the child had committed to excite her so. A smug justification hung around the fringes of his vision and then it fell hard to the ground as he felt her laugh break the sound barrier and deafen his senses. He watched mesmerized. Instead of a curly haired quarter-cast quasso, he saw Alex, his sandy hair tousled and free, smiling up at her playful antics as they danced and celebrated. What was she about? He willed himself away and turned his horse for home.

৵•෬

Maggie caught a movement on the top of the bank that rose up behind the river, as the back of a horse-rider turned and disappeared over the rise. Tom looked at her flushed face and shrugged. "That be the Boss Captain. He ain't no good when it comes to shadow'n. We know he been there all the time."

"He was watching us? For how long?"

"Na, I was watching him... since I been here."

"Shadow, may I walk home with you? I would like to pay my respects to your Father. It's time for me to leave Henderson's Gap. I'll be going away very soon."

Tom offered Maggie his arm and helped her over the uneven ground. There was no doubt Jones had done well with his son. He was a good kid. Maggie reached down and adjusted her shoe. She spotted a flawless pair of dove-grey smooth stone-skippers lying by her feet and tucked them in her pinafore. Tom chatted and spoke with pride about a horse he was going to have one day, soon – when he was ten... and how his sisters annoyed him with their silliness. He talked about some of the hunts Blondie had taken him on and how he was learning to 'track as good as him'.

They came to the worker's cottage and Shadow disappeared. Maggie paused and then tentatively knocked on the door jam. She spotted a cowbell hanging there and jangled it by the rope. She wondered if Tom lived with his father or his mistress-mother. Silence. She turned to go when Jones strode through the gate beside the cottage. "Miss Maggie, good to see you! Young Tom said you were visiting. Please come around the back. Olivia is cooking a roast for dinner. We do that outside, but there's no reason we can't visit at the same time..."

Olivia? That's right. She remembered now. She was grateful Jones had courteously prompted her about his wife's name. No help for the Foreman's household either. Life was as self-supporting here as it was for the house-staff at the homestead. Not at all like Fairfield Estate. She followed him around the side of the cottage. It was small and compact and even with the detached kitchen being commandeered for other purposes; it would still be cramped for a family with six kids.

The back part of the hut was hedged in with paperbark, grevillea and callistemon trees creating a sort of private courtyard, expanding out into a larger yard. In the centre were half logs set in a semi-circle around an open fireplace and a stone-set bush oven. Bark and gum leaves carpeted the area creating a soft sound as Maggie walked over them. Olivia was bundled over the fireplace deep in work until Jones gently placed his hand on her shoulder. She stood up and stretched and turned to make her guest feel welcome. Maggie paused as Olivia extended a slender dark-skinned hand accompanied with a broad white-toothed smile.

Maggie stared. The black woman? She knew Jones had been friendly with a half-cast from the local mob. But wife? He married *her*? Maggie looked up to see Tom standing in a line of *quasso* kids curiously looking at this lady visiting from the Big House. Maggie dropped her hand and turned away. Jones quietly stepped up. "Maggie, this is my wife, Olivia. Liv, this is Maggie – Lonnie and Sammy's charge who has come home after being the prodigal for... whoa, must be nigh ten or so years. It is good to have you home Maggie. It has been a long time."

"You *married* her?"

"Yes. You left just before our wedding. It's all official: Henderson endorsed our application with the Aboriginal Protection Board. She is my wife Maggie. I won't be pretending that managing people's reactions has been easy. I love her."

Maggie stared at him and looked at the faces of the kids lined up before her. Jones introduced them by name: "Priscilla, Jemimah, Tom, Keziah and Andy - they are twins. And this is little Keren. You know... Priscilla is named after her grandmother... my mum was a Godly, generous woman. Job in the Bible was a man who lost everything and then God gave him three beautiful daughters... Jemimah, Keziah and Keren... smart as well... princesses in their Kingdom. Thomas and Andrew were men God used to change nations. God has blessed our family."

Maggie stared at them, speechless. Tom gaped openly, challenging her hesitation. Why was she more comfortable with the idea that Tom was his bastard half-cast than his legitimate son? She closed her eyes, to regain her balance and her manners. "Missus Jones, please forgive my intrusion. I wanted to meet the

Jones family before I leave Henderson's Gap. It is a pleasure to meet you all."

She extended her hand again and Olivia gently took the peace offering. Maggie had not been the only one surprised that Marshal Jones had taken a wife with Aboriginal blood. "Please... call me Liv."

Jones poured her a mug of tea and handed it to her as the kids dispersed. "You goin' back to the city then?"

Maggie laughed softly as she took a seat on the logs set around the fire. "No. I can't bring myself to do that yet. I've had an inkling to pursue another direction, but I will have to see what becomes available." An idea glowed in her mind. "It is something I am very keen to try..."

Jones studied his boots and paused. "So, the thing with the Captain's boy – Alex... that didn't work out?"

"Actually, Alexander and I got along famously. There were... other complications." She smiled wryly. "It must be the shortest engagement as a governess in history... something like ten minutes! I had the audacity to resign, otherwise, I'd be smarting from the humiliation of being let go." She paused and looked at Jones. "I remembered something you said once: 'Pain with a purpose'. Funnily enough, it has given me a conviction of the direction I want to try." She smiled to herself. It sounded like she had all the freedoms of the landed gentry and could do whatever she wanted.

Oh well. Her option was not to go back to Aunt Winifred's. Her Aunt had been generous, but her season for being there was over. She knew that now. "I want to governess," she said lightly. Then she hesitated as she registered a profound silence to her nattering. She had a tendency to say too much when she was nervous. Jones wasn't her self-appointed confessional priest anymore, but she knew the authentic word-of-mouth bush telegraph still worked efficiently. She studied her hands and launched ahead anyway. "I wanted to ask... Perhaps you know of a family around abouts... someone who is looking to engage a governess? I am now officially on the hunt for a position. I didn't want to go too far afield, with Lonnie and Sammy here."

When she looked up, she saw Jones and Olivia's eyes locked in an unspoken conversation. It almost took Maggie's breath away. The call of a peewee chimed out in the trees around their courtyard, echoing their own private magpie-lark duet. Maggie gapped unabashed, and then looked away when Jones cleared his throat. He was studying his boots again. Maggie flinched at her intrusion. "Oh, I'm sorry. I have really taken a liberty to ask. It was way too familiar. Please forgive me..."

"Nah Miss Maggie, you were always one to speak your mind. Actually, Liv knows of a position..." His words hung tantalizingly in the air. She knew he said it deliberately. Testing her willingness to accept his wife;

accept his family; accept his choices. Maggie looked at him, taking up the challenge. Even if she didn't know Olivia, she knew Jones. Jones she could trust.

Maggie looked from one to the other. Olivia hesitated shyly. "There is a place looking for a teacher to start a provisional school for the worker's kids. The Bosses' would still have a private governess I guess, but these kids have no one. We would like to suggest this position for you."

Maggie blinked. "A school? Are you serious? That sounds amazing!" Suddenly she paused. "Would they even consider me? I'm a ten-minute wonder," she said with a grin.

Jones cleared his throat again. "Haven't been able to find a teacher yet. They have approval about wages and a classroom. It seems all set to go on the proviso they can find a suitable candidate, but it has been harder than anyone thought. Would you consider putting in a letter of application?"

Olivia shifted and went back to her fire. Excitement rippled through Maggie's voice. "Do you really think I could? I mean... well, to start with, it's a teacher's position. What about the Board of General Education? It still is not so common for women..." This was an unbelievable opportunity.

When Olivia sat down again, she gave Jones a significant look. "Marshall, tell her," she said.

Maggie looked from one to the other, unspoken words giving her a twang in her chest. Leon would never look at her that way. Jones cleared his throat and sighed. "The school is for here: at Henderson's Gap. The students would be from here and surrounding places. The Board of General Education have needed fifteen students to start official enrolments... but they recently re-evaluated the criteria so provisional schools can open with just twelve kids. At the moment there are eleven kids who aren't getting schooling – formal like, but we would include our little Keren to make up the numbers... she's turning four later in the year. The school is non-vested... a private one, so we have a level of control with a few provisos from the Board of General Education – they fund the teacher. With your schooling, you are more than adequately qualified for what we are looking for. Really, all we want is for our kids not to miss out. I do what I can, but it's hard to keep it consistent when working long hours. We've been praying about this and the idea of a school – and starting with this non-vested arrangement seems a way. As the enrolments increase, the Board may place a permanent teacher. We talked to Henderson before he left and he gave it the go-ahead. It's pretty much been left to me to finalize."

"So, you get to approve the 'suitable candidate'? Then there shouldn't be a problem!"

Jones shook his head, quietly showing some reservation. "Well no... The Captain has been given oversight. He's talked about a school committee, but I think, at this stage – he is it."

Maggie sighed. "Well, I can tell you right now, there is no way he will even consider me. I would hate to get your hopes up and have him blockade it from every angle."

Olivia chuckled. "What did you do to him? Must have been an impressive ten minutes."

Maggie shrugged. "I'm not going to ask him for a reference, much less expect endorsement to teach here. As appealing as this is, and as much as I would love to be the one to start this for you, I think you are going to have to find another teacher. I am so sorry." Well – she was sorry about that, but not about the Captain.

Jones shrugged. "We have to try. I believe you're our teacher. Let God deal with the Captain. Just keep your letter generic, and don't put your name on it. I can say I've interviewed and am happy. He hasn't seemed greatly interested really. It might be enough."

Maggie stood to leave. She smiled mischievously, "I'll give you the letter tomorrow. If you can get it past him, I'm more than willing." A royal decree, sealed in wax from the Queen herself, would be easier in her opinion. Still, these people were praying believers in miracles. Their quiet confidence made it almost seem possible.

Maggie paced. She had gone outside and found herself down by the river. What she felt inside was very different to anything she had experienced before. Unlike the night when she had tossed with a plethora of creative inspirations crowding her mind, this was a burning, a deep-seated anxiety. She could not remember a time, ever, when she had wanted something so much it hurt. Suddenly, almost without expecting it, this was staring at her, tantalizing her, luring her, and hanging out of reach.

Jones' confidence echoed in her ears. Olivia's shy smile quietly spoke of a mother's yearning for her kids to excel in a bi-cultural world. What they wanted was unusual. Yet they weren't angry; they weren't militant; they weren't distressed; they weren't pacing down by the river. How could that be?

She pictured Jones just staring at his boots, cracked and worn. Maggie recalled a night when they were sitting by the fire. Maggie had teased Jones about his fascination with his ugly boots. He had smiled and said, "I don't mind that they're ugly – it reminds me..." Maggie was not in the mood to play his game that night, where he would run ideas around until she chased them down, so he simply told her.

"The steps of a good man are ordered by the LORD: and he delighteth in his way. Though he fall, he shall not be utterly cast down: for the LORD upholdeth him with his

hand... Delight thyself also in the LORD; and he shall give thee the desires of thine heart. Commit thy way unto the LORD; trust also in him; and he shall bring it to pass."

"I'm just reminding myself God's got it in hand; He's got me in hand. I just keep committing my steps and way to the Lord. He don't mind that my boots are worn and ugly... just the same to Him as your pretty dancing shoes. He just wants them committed. Are your steps committed to Him, Maggie?"

Maggie stopped and stared at her black dress boots. How was it she had found her way back here after all this time? Was it because she had once committed her steps to God, and He had not let go? It felt like she had walked away. Not intentionally of course, but a step here, and a step there... until she looked back and she was nowhere near where she used to be. A deep sadness swept through her. There had been a time when she felt so close to God's heart. She hesitated. How far would she take this? As a child, it had been easy – like putting her hand through Sammy's long arm and trotting along to keep pace with his gangly stride. God had been her friend. The One she told every secret to. All that seemed so long ago; so simple; so satisfying.

She walked out onto a gravelly sand bar on the bend in the river and sat down on a log embedded in the gravel. This school – what if this school was His answer to Jones and Liv's prayers? "Oh God, don't let the Captain blockade their dream." Did she believe divine resources could give them everything they needed to make it work? She wanted it to work... but more than that... she wanted to be the one who did it. She picked up a pebble and splashed it in the water. Splintered colours reflected off the water, and she realized her steps were held in the hands of the Master. If this anticipation that burned so hot in her belly did not work out, then perhaps God would give her a different way to see it fulfilled, or snuff the burning out. She had to believe that. Because one thing she did know: she was sure she could not live with it, not like this; not for long. It would corrode her sanity.

•

The Captain looked over the page and paused when he got to the part about three consecutive rowing championships. "So, the fellow is fit and competitive. Would he be happy with such a back-block position? No disrespect to your little tykes Jones, but it doesn't seem like a job for anyone with a scrap of ambition, wanting to go somewhere."

Jones grinned. "You and me both know ambition comes in many forms. For a young person starting out, this provides experience, challenge, variety. Henderson's Gap has a frontier feel. That appeals, particularly to someone looking to stretch their legs outside the city."

"City slicker then. Will he be able to cut it, do you think? Don't really want to be revisiting this next month because he couldn't hack the lack of social life."

"Seemed keen enough. We'll do what we can to soften the blow."

The Captain looked at Jones grimly. "This is the only applicant you've found, isn't it?" Jones nodded honestly. The Captain shrugged. "Well, should be good to go."

"Should?" Jones grinned. "Or we can do this, definitely?"

"Yes – he is yours. Sign for a year. We'll review after that."

"You beauty!" Jones couldn't keep the excitement out of his voice as he put papers out on the desk. "I have all the conditions we discussed – I'll get the other signature and bring the originals back to you as soon as I can. Don't want this one to get away."

The Captain reviewed the list and signed without pause. He was happy to have this sorted at last. Alex was still young, and Thelma covered the basics. He didn't *have* to have a governess or tutor just yet, but he would like to have that settled as well. If this fellow worked out, he might be able to do private lessons.

❧ • ❧

Maggie's heart leapt as she heard Jones' whoop from inside the library. It was okay. Relief swept through her veins warming her skin. She took a deep breath. Keep it together; be cool. Don't let on. Don't sabotage yourself now it has progressed this far. She wiped her sweaty palms on her skirt and waited, holding a gift-wrapped box in her hand.

Finally, the library door opened, and Jones stood there beaming. A flicker of unease flashed across his eyes as he looked at her, wondering why she was here. "Miss Maggie, it is a fine day today!" he said, loaded with meaning.

Maggie relaxed as she saw his boyish grin. "Yes, Jones… it is," she responded warmly, her eyes reflecting his excitement. "I'm just here to see if I can catch a moment with your manager." Jones reached out and squeezed her shoulder and left. Maggie looked up to see the Captain staring at her. "Sir, if you have a moment…"

"I will not reconsider your resignation." He had just signed on a teacher. He felt his position of control. He didn't need to negotiate.

"Really? You think I am here to beg for more of your *charity*? You don't have to reconsider anything Sir, because I certainly have not! As I recall, I merely requested a *moment* of your time. However,…" She stopped and took a deep breath. The man unnerved her. Try again. Be civil. "Please. Sir, I have a farewell gift for Alexander…"

"Oh." That was unexpected.

She stepped into the library. "Alexander was upset when I told him about our decision. As I am not to continue as his governess, I wanted to give him something – just a small gift. With your permission of course."

"*Our* decision? I believed *you* resigned your appointment."

"True. I did. But you cannot challenge that the outcome was mutually agreeable and ultimately inevitable."

He swallowed. "So, what did you want?"

"Well, given your doubts regarding me, I wanted permission to visit Alexander to give him the gift. Or, I suppose you could accompany me." She hoped against that option. "Or, you could just give it to him yourself, although it is a bit complicated and I would like the opportunity to explain it to him."

He blinked and looked at the gift-box in her hand. He thought it trembled slightly. "He's just upstairs." Normally he would dismiss such a request and be satisfied with Thelma's presence in the room, but the vision of her dancing by the riverside made him curious. "It shouldn't take a moment. We can go now if you like."

"I... thank you," she murmured. She felt her heart sink. She really didn't want him as her audience. He walked around from behind his desk and opened the door, standing back with a gentlemanly bow. She stepped through the door with a most intriguing sensation rising in her chest as she passed by him. Her hands gripped the wrapping tightly.

As he escorted her towards the staircase a weird feeling washed over her. As she quietly mounted the stairs, a feeling like being announced as the Belle-of-the-Ball surrounded her like a haze. She walked, step by step, waiting for the aura surrounding this moment to pop, fizzle and vaporize. He paused before he knocked at the nursery door and looked down at her. She inhaled quickly and looked away, holding her breath for a moment. 'He feels it too', she thought to herself in panic. 'I know he feels it too.' All she could think to say was "Will Alexander be very upset, do you think?"

He had not taken his eyes off her face, tracing every line, trying to unravel the puzzle. "We'll see," he said quietly, and he opened the door and stood back. Maggie stepped inside. "Alexander," she said quietly with a beautiful smile and she coloured slightly as she wasn't sure whom the smile was for. She was glad her back was towards the door.

Alex looked up from the blocks where he was playing, and his eyes lit up. "Miss Maggie! You came! Can we spend the day together after all?"

She came forward as he jumped up. "My champion! Look what you are doing here! How clever you are!" She sat on the floor beside him and added a block to his structure. "Alexander, I had a really lovely time with you the other day. Unfortunately, we are still not going to have time together like we thought, so I wanted to give you something to remind you of what we did. Is that okay?"

He looked at her seriously and glanced towards the door uncertainly. What he saw must have reassured him as he nodded. She pulled the package from behind her back and gave it to him. "This is for you, but inside is something for me..." Maggie said mysteriously. He opened the wrapping and there was a writing set box. It had been a present she had bought for Leon, but the rough-hewn timber just didn't seem like something that went with his engraved ivory-handled paper-knife. She had put it in her bag, perhaps to give to Sammy, but he really wasn't a writer either. Alex opened the lid and studied the set, baffled. Maggie showed him the nibs. "We didn't get to do any writing, but one day you will. This set will be good to use then," Maggie said. "But we did do one thing together..." and she handed him another package from inside the box. Alex ripped open the paper and a big smile lit up his face. He held in his hand two dove-grey skipping stones and mimicked them skipping across the carpet.

"This one is for you, and this one is for me..." she reminded him. "Let me read it to you..." She had attached a little message on a card: "*May you always defy gravity and skip where others sink...*" She turned it over and it was simply signed ~ *Miss Maggie*. "I want you to remember our day. The words seem a little complicated now, but one day you will understand them." She drew him in for a hug.

"And this one is mine, and I want you to draw your face on the card for me... with your writing set, so I can remember you." She set the nib and loaded it with ink, gently guiding his hand as he wobbled some eyes and a mouth. On the back of the card, his hand trembled the shape of an "A". She looked at it proudly when he had finished and held it up to his face to see the likeness. "Look – you are smiling! Thank you, Alexander, it is lovely." It was crooked and perfect. She had made him smile. She blew on the ink to help it dry and stood to her feet as she said goodbye. Her eyes were a little misty while she walked to the door holding her treasure carefully so not to smudge it. She stopped as the Captain looked at her mystified. "Thank you, Sir. I appreciate that very much."

5.

Maggie waited until after dinner when she was confident the Captain would be buried in the Library attending to his ledgers. She went down to Jones's hut, and quietly jangled the cowbell. She jumped as a dog barked, and again when Olivia opened the door to invite her inside. The cottage was small, sparse and tidy. Bunk beds lined the walls of one bedroom, a tangle of curly hair on each pillow. The other was the main bedroom, with a crib jammed in the corner. The sitting room was small and Jones was at a table wedged against the wall. Olivia smiled. "Could never quite get the hang of living all inside. I like seeing the sky when we eat. Just as well, given how small this place is."

Jones stood to his feet as they came in. "Miss Maggie, I believe you are now our new teacher. Congratulations." He handed her the sheets and she sat down and read through the terms. She stopped when she got to the end. His signature stood out on the page, bold and confident: *Duncan McCray*. The man everyone referred to, as *Captain* was actually a Mr McCray. She looked at it for some time, absorbing his identity. Mr McCray, Duncan, Mr Duncan McCray.

"So, what did he say when you told him it was me?"

Jones' eyes had a mischievous glint and his mouth twisted in a sheepish grin. "Actually, I didn't. And he didn't ask."

"He signed on an unnamed teacher? Just like that?"

"The resume was impressive enough. His main concern was that a *fellow* with those credentials might not stick it out."

Maggie took a deep breath and lifted up her pen. "Well then," she said with a grin, and slowly she let out her breath as she signed under his name, relieved now it was in writing. The subterfuge frightened her a little. She was pretty sure there would be major seismic activity when Mister McCray found out the name of their new teacher. She raised her brow slightly. She had an advantage. She had learned his name first.

Jones grimaced. Was it lying not to correct some very obvious assumptions? He had painfully chosen his words. He had never actually *said* anything false. He would just have to go into damage control when it all erupted, but not yet. "Henderson agreed to the use of the old stockmen's quarters for the schoolhouse and teacher's place. It's not much... but we have the whole building. I've been working on cleaning it out but was mainly waiting 'til we found a teacher to see what they would want. Now you are here, I'd like you to take a look. When do you think we can begin lessons?" His thoughts tumbled over each other.

Maggie sat back and took a deep breath. "I have no idea. I have never been a teacher. How long will it take to have the schoolroom ready to start? That's really all it depends on. It doesn't have to be perfect... and we will keep working on it. That's all written here anyway," she said referring to the documents on the table. She sat up – her eyes bright. "Could we have a look now? I hardly remember what it is like."

Jones unhooked the lantern from its stand and they walked to the quarters in the fading dusk. They were dusty and old – just six rooms joined by a verandah. "Now my thinking was we convert three rooms for your living quarters and we join the other rooms for the schoolroom."

Maggie stood outside on the verandah and quietly let her mind float with visions. She looked inside in the fading light, excitement rising. This was real. It was actually happening. A tear rolled down her cheek, as she stood amazed by the tangible evidence of this surreal dream. It had happened so fast; it took her breath away... a bit like being tipped out of a canoe in the river on an icy morning. Maggie's voice cracked with emotion. "I have so many ideas running around my head just now. Can I come over tomorrow and run through them?"

Jones visibly sighed with relief. "Thanks, Maggie – It's good of you not to despise this humble set-up.

Even with all your learning, this is not above you. I appreciate that. Tomorrow we make a start on your plan."

"Our plan," corrected Maggie as they walked down the stairs. She paused slightly. "Jones, when do you think it will be a good time to tell the Captain who the new teacher is?"

He shrugged. "Kinda thinking there isn't going to be a good time. We'll just have to pray there isn't much blood spilt. Let's say for now that you're giving me advice – a woman's angle, on what we're doing... which is true. He may not even ask. So, I'll see you here first thing in the morning?"

જ઼•ન્જ઼

Maggie walked home in a daze. This would have to go down in her diary as the most nerve-wrenching day of her life. For the next year – all going well, she would have eleven... twelve little people to teach... and to top it off, a schoolhouse to call her own. How extraordinary. It never occurred to her to think she may be way in over her level of expertise or experience. The fire in her belly burned bright. These kids will be given every opportunity to learn, to grow and expand and fill out their God-given potential... and laugh. When she got to her room, she pulled some paper from her writing set. She sat down and started to draw what she had seen. Suddenly plans flowed freely and she mapped out her ideas. Tomorrow she could start to see flesh added to the bones of this dream. She sighed. She couldn't have been happier.

∂•∾

Maggie scrubbed the floor in the rooms that were going to be her private lodgings with a stiff bristle brush. She was on all fours and working her way around the skirting board. She had shown Jones her sketches and they pulled down the dividing walls to create the classroom. He had workmen dragging away rubbish, patching up shutters and mending floorboards on the verandah. Timber was being recycled to make desks and forms for the children to sit on. A chalkboard had been ordered from town and the long grass was slashed with a scythe. It was a working-bee on an impressive scale and Maggie was astounded at the progress being made. The walls were given a fresh coat of milk-paint inside and out; and the verandah was brightened with a splash of cobalt blue along the rails.

Maggie had been working alongside the men for days and she was stiff and tired. A temporary copper had been set up and the fire was stoked for a steady supply of hot water. Everything had been scrubbed with hot water and carbolic soap. Already the tangy, tarry smell gave it a wholesome, clean feel. Maggie's hair flopped in her face, flushed with exertion, as she finished the last of the floors. Every muscle ached as she pushed herself without mercy. She stood to her feet to stretch and tossed the cold, murky water in her bucket over the rail. She shrieked in horror as she realized, too late, that someone was standing in her line of disposal. In a desperate attempt to avoid drenching them, she spun back. The bucket sloshed again, and in an instant, she was also soaked in filthy water from head to toe. She stood momentarily frozen, her back towards her victim; half aware that she was not the only one wet, and fully aware of every workman on Henderson's Gap staring at her grubby dress and saturated hair. The exhaustion washed over her and a fatigued laugh bubbled from the back of her throat. "Guess I couldn't wait to have a bath. This is very hot work!" She turned to apologize for her poor choice of dumping point and stared, mortified, into the wet face of the Captain. Her laughter drained from her, along with the colour from her face. "Oh goodness! I am so sorry Sir!" she whispered mortified. His expressionless gaze held her stare.

Very slowly he reached inside his vest pocket and then wiped his face with a kerchief. He turned on his heel and left her staring after him. "That woman is a complete disaster," he muttered as he strode past Jones, and he wasn't certain, but Jones was pretty sure he detected the makings of an amused twist on his lips.

🕐•🕐

Maggie lay in the hip-bath Lonnie had drawn for her. Tears sprinkled her lashes. Could anything be more humiliating? Lonnie sat at the head of the tub massaging her scalp as she lathered her hair, muttering away in Mandarin as she did. "Missy, *Lou Mou* listens to your heart."

Maggie swiped her eyes. "Oh *Lou Mou*, this is a mess! Could anything else go wrong? The man is like a bad penny!"

Lonnie grunted. Finally, someone agreed with her.

Maggie slid under the suds and resurfaced slowly. "What was I thinking? I won't be able to run a school if I have to work within three hundred miles of him."

Lonnie offered a very pragmatic shrug as she poured a pitcher of warm water and rinsed her hair. "It not so hard. I work, he work, I don't get in his way; he don't get in Lonnie's way."

Maggie sat upright. "It's not just him. I really want this to work. I want to stay here a while... to be with you and Sammy. I had to go away last time. I never came to visit. They didn't understand what it was like here. I think part of me was really scared I would never be able to leave if I came back during term holidays. I don't want to go. I just want to be home!"

"You are home Missy. You right. I glad you home. You live long, long way down at schoolhouse.

There lot of space. Not three hundred miles… but there be lot of space between you and the Captain. It will be okay."

Maggie wondered about that. Every fibre in her body tensed until Lonnie started massaging again. She leaned back against the towel-padded metal and closed her eyes. "I'm not so sure Henderson's Gap is big enough. God, I don't see how this is going to work!"

❧•❧

The Captain handed back the duplicate sheets of paper to Jones. "Happy with all that…" he said. He paused, changing track. "When do you expect the teacher to start lessons?"

Jones looked at him thoughtfully. "Week after next."

"Hmm, so when is he arriving?"

He avoided that. "The work on the rooms is progressing well. Expecting to have everything moved in by Friday."

"Oh? As soon as that. So, could you pass on an invitation then? Dinner at the main house on Saturday night? Might seem hospitable for an appointment such as this. Been a while since I've indulged a good port and cigar after dinner."

Jones considered that for a moment. He cleared his throat. "Captain, I think you should know… the 'him' is a 'her'."

"What do you mean, 'him is a her'? He's not of dubious character, is he?"

"No Captain, straight as a die, I believe. It's just he's not a man. The teacher's a woman."

The Captain blinked. "Oh. A woman? As in *skirts*?" When Jones nodded slowly, he sighed. "Oh. Like a nun?"

The idea of Maggie being a nun made him smile. "Don't believe so Captain. Just a teacher."

"Hmmm. Well, that puts a dampener on the whole port-and-cigars after-dinner ritual, doesn't it? Think we'd just better call it off."

"Up to you Captain. It would be a polite gesture though. She is still the new teacher after all," he offered with a touch of mischief in his eyes.

"Do you think?" The idea of a man's world being encroached on by a woman left him feeling ill at ease. The Captain closed his eyes feeling uncharacteristically awkward. Even a matronly schoolma'am was unsettling. Another thought hit him with panic. "What on earth would we talk about?"

"Just keep it to the school, Captain. That should be safe."

He sighed, resigned. "Very well Jones." Then he suddenly added, "Would you be free to come? Moral support?" Jones nodded. He really didn't want to miss this. The Captain got up and walked around his chair to the window. "The teacher is really a woman? How could I miss that?" He sounded quite bewildered.

Jones followed his gaze outside, across the fence to the tree line. "I didn't really make a concerted effort to correct the misunderstanding Captain."

"Humph. That's evident." He shrugged and gave a short snort. "I would like the security of having another female present. Then I wouldn't have to say too much. Is Maggie still around? I'd be inclined to ask her to come."

Jones grinned widely. Oh, he was enjoying this. "You'd be a brave man – you could end up wearing your soup!"

The Captain gave a low laconic laugh. "I would guarantee it."

Jones looked the other way and turned to leave. "Hey Jones, that whole thing about horse-riding, you know... the equestrian and rowing championships... that was all concocted to make the application read well: a good spiel, right?"

"No Captain, as far as I know, I believe that was all fair dinkum."

6.

Maggie tied the ribbon on the bodice of her dress as Lonnie fussed with her petticoat. "If I don't come out of this alive, bury me down by the river. The river-gums and koalas can sing dirges at my funeral."

Lonnie clicked her tongue and huffed, "Don't talk nonsense Missy. You will be fine."

Maggie applied some lip-wax. She was still undecided how important this evening dinner-appointment was. Truly, she had no idea. If she were starting at any other establishment it would be a big deal. She just couldn't shake the sensation she was walking into a fire. The fact Jones would be there too alleviated the heat a little, but she knew they could both end up fried or fired.

Jones had more to lose than her. His family, his house, his job, his whole life... it was all tied up in Henderson's Gap. She, at least, was invested in just a single desperate desire. She stood beside the stove in the kitchen waiting for Jones. She rolled her shoulders – and felt the adrenaline in her body surge as it did just before a race. It began to rain. Jones stomped on the back stairs and pushed open the door. His hair damp, dripping onto the collar of his best Sunday shirt.

"Well, ain't you a sight for sore eyes Miss Maggie! We'll have half our men wanting to go back to school. Learning could become quite the new thing." He glanced at her face. "So... ready?"

Maggie smiled and rolled her eyes a little. "Can you ever be ready for a firing squad?"

"Still want to arrive at the front entrance? Could be a whole lot dryer just stepping through the house."

"This teacher is not going to meet her employer by walking through a scullery. I prefer to get wet." He raised his eyebrows and offered her his arm. She clutched it hard and was hit by a wave of clarity. This was ludicrous. How could she teach children? But then the powerful driving within her propelled her forward. She had never needed to fight for anything before. This was different because it was important. She took a breath, resolutely preparing for battle. The rain-shower had eased to the finest of drizzles.

Maggie pulled up her skirts and scampered along the damp path around the side of the house, jumping a puddle of accumulated water where the pavers had sunk. She bounded up the sweeping front steps to the wide double doors. The coloured glass panelling looked charming as the candelabra inside the entrance twinkled a greeting. Maggie wondered what it would be like coming here for the first time. For her this was familiar. Nothing had really changed from when she was growing up, only back then she had never been allowed to use "The Big Door".

Jones clanged the knocker and stood back. Maggie could see Sammy through the glass pane, in his white collared shirt and waistcoat, coming to open the door. Courteously he bowed and placed a settling hand on her arm, and as they went inside, he leaned over and whispered, "I've got the shotgun under the side-board in case things get ugly."

Maggie couldn't help herself. She laughed. "Oh Sammy, I love you! But I don't think it will be necessary."

Just then the Captain appeared in his jacket, formal and smart – his brass buttons blinked at her. Maggie wondered if he realized she had pressed those creases on his sleeves this afternoon so Lonnie could put her feet up for a moment. He didn't seem at all surprised at her being here. Did he already know? Was everything settled?

"What won't be necessary?" the Captain asked innocently, determined to master small talk for this evening.

"The shotgun under the sideboard."

"Oh." He paused and looked at her charming smile. Really? Never mind, she was obviously teasing. "Anyway, thanks Jones for asking Maggie to join us. I'm sure the conversation will be easier with another lady at the table. Trust I have not delayed your plans, Maggie, by coming out tonight?"

"No, thank you... everything is fine. Although I am unsettled and motivated by everything at the same time." Sammy faded into the background and the three stood in the foyer momentarily. Maggie was playing unconsciously with the frill on her cuff. The Captain looked away and then looked back at her. The colour of her dress did incredible things to her hair, dusted with fine droplets of rain that glinted like diamantes in the candlelight.

"Oh. So, you've found a new position?"

Huh. So, he still hadn't joined the dots. "Yes. Quite simply it seems. I'm excited by this opportunity – it has quite exceeded my expectations."

"Oh," he said again. He brushed his forehead with the palm of his hand. "Please, let's wait in the sitting room. Dinner will be served as soon as we are all here."

"Are you expecting many guests?" Perhaps this was bigger than she had understood.

"No just a small party. Us... and ahh, the new teacher of course." He flicked at his collar. It had been a while since he'd been in formal wear, and he'd forgotten to check the teacher's name. Never mind, the introductions would have to sort that.

As they moved inside, Maggie twisted her eyes at Jones, who was determined not to make eye contact. She turned and saw the Captain had witnessed her contortions, so she made a point of glancing around the room with an appreciative eye. "You know, it is different – seeing a house as a guest and not as 'home'. It alters the way you experience it – it has a different feel." She caressed the polished wood on the back of a settee. A visitor didn't have to dust the fittings. The Captain watched her hand intrigued, like he didn't quite know what to do with it – whether he wanted to stomp on it and kill it, or pick it up and hold it.

"So, this new appointment – it seems to have taken the edge off the brevity of your previous... engagement?" He groaned inwardly. Why couldn't he leave it alone? It's just that he was so curious to know where she was going, what she was doing since... but he also didn't want her storming out just yet. He had dinner to get through. He didn't stop to analyse why he assumed a dramatic exit would be the inevitable outcome of any conversation with her.

Maggie lifted her eyes and looked directly into his. She hadn't realized they were so dark, so grey. She held his gaze in defiance. "I will *never* say I am not disappointed in the way that went. I believe you know that is the case and it is unfair to suggest otherwise."

Jones raised his eyebrows and turned away to pour a round of drinks so they wouldn't see his amusement. The Captain looked at her steadily. "My only inference was disappointment could be alleviated by new challenges. Nothing more."

"Oh, believe me, this will be a challenge."

"Then, 'to challenges'. A drink..." he said, and he handed her a glass. He was determined to be the pleasant host. Five years in hiding was enough. He really had lost his social prowess. He looked at the clock on the mantle and then checked the watch in his pocket as he sat down on the lounge.

Maggie looked at the glass in her hand and quickly took a drink. She wondered how long they could politely wait for someone to arrive who was already here. She picked at the lint on the settee and tried to catch a glimpse of Jones. She had no idea how to proceed. Awkwardly she cleared her throat. "Sir, I feel I must..." and the front door knocker clanged loudly. The Captain got up with relief. "Excuse me... that must be our company. Now we can serve dinner... Sammy!" Maggie and Jones looked at each other mystified. "Let's make our way to the dining-room, Sammy can escort our guest there." The Captain offered his arm to Maggie. 'You were saying?"

She momentarily hesitated and suddenly felt disorientated. She remembered the last time she walked by his side. She glanced at his face and he stared straight ahead. Perhaps she had been mistaken. Perhaps he had not sensed what she had felt... or was feeling. It was there again. A weird, ethereal sensation fluttered around the fringe of her vision... and it made her feel she could glide like an angel. Her pause caused him to look at her, searching as if he too was looking for a clue. "Come, dinner will be served," is all he said, and they walked out ahead of Jones.

The Captain pulled out a dining chair for Maggie, and she settled, thanking him with a glorious smile. She was chatting pleasantly. She was aware that whatever this was, it was elevating her mind and her feelings. It was a relief almost, taking away the fear and the pain, numbing the nervousness and helping her to be the teacher she felt this man would expect. Easily he joined in with a story and she laughed. For the first time, Maggie saw him smile, comfortable and amiable.

After a while, he glanced at the door and frowned slightly. He paused then and hesitated, as if he should see what the delay was, but not wanting to move. A silent thought floated through his mind, as he swirled the wine in his glass. Then Sammy appeared at the door. "Sir, allow me to introduce Mister Hastings – Mister Leon Hastings." As he stepped aside, Hastings came through the door with a sweep of his hand. "Thanks, Sammy..." he said mildly.

The Captain was on his feet in a moment. "Good grief, can't we make up our minds? First, there's a chap coming; then I'm told it's a woman... and now you stand there, obviously a gentleman. Entirely better for me though – port and cigars to round off our meal after all! If that's okay with you? Take a seat Sir... and welcome."

Leon looked a little bemused but chuckled agreeably. "Anything that ends with fine port and a quality cigar has got to be a good thing," he said. He pulled out a chair and sat easily beside a white-faced Maggie as Sammy laid another setting.

The music in Maggie's head came to a screeching, squealing halt. Her mind froze and her chatter evaporated. But neither the Captain nor Hastings seemed to notice. They nattered like old friends. Soon they were on to social hunting and sports, speaking the same language from another life, antidotes flowing with the smoothness of the fine wine they were drinking.

Jones looked at Maggie curiously and wondered at her obvious discomfiture. He scrutinized the dynamic between the two at the head of the table. Had the Captain made another appointment, one which suited his sense of social class better? *Be sure your sins will find you out*, he firmly sermonized inside his head. But then, they had her position in writing and signed. Already Maggie's things had been moved into the schoolrooms. He looked at the fine cut of Hasting's jacket and couldn't picture this man teaching his kids... any kids.

They made their way through soup, and then the main course of succulent roast duck was served. Lonnie's cooking was beyond excellent; every preferred detail attended to. The Captain commended the delicious menu a number of times, but Maggie barely touched her food. She felt sick to the pit of her stomach. Turmoil swirled around her like a psychedelic haze. Eventually, she placed her serviette on her plate and pushed her chair out. "Excuse me, gentlemen, I do not feel well. I will have to take some fresh air." She ran to the front door and out onto the sweeping verandah. The rain had started again, and she paced, up and down, gulping the rain-washed air as if someone was trying to strangle her. What was he doing here? He had no right!

Jones followed her out and watched Maggie's anxious face doused with dread at every turn of her pacing. He stepped forward gently. "Maggie?" She turned and barely registered he was there. "Maggie? What has happened? Who is this man?"
Maggie stopped and looked at him as he quietly repeated, "Who is he?"

"His name is Leon Hastings. I... he... we... know each other."

"Well, I gathered as much. Exactly how do you know him?"

"Everyone was expecting we would be engaged, but well, obviously we are not."

Jones stood there. "Oh. The "big house" guy. You knew him pretty well then. I gather this engagement is not entirely ancient history. Was it...?" He left the question hanging.

"Me. I broke it off. Well, I didn't... exactly... formally. Actually, I ran."

So that's why she came home. "And now you regret that?"

"No... yes... No. No. I know it was right... but..."

"But?"

Maggie looked up at Jones, his honest eyes frank with concern. "Oh Jones, I don't think I will be able to take the position now."

"And that would be because...?" said Jones, confused.

"Because... because of him! Oh, what evil ever inspired him to turn up here?"

"Come Maggie – what are you talking about? Is the man an axe murderer?"

Maggie stared at him horrified. "No... Nothing like that! It's just..." How could he ever comprehend? He and Olivia had an uncommonly blessed understanding. She ran down the stairs and out into the rain.

❦•❧

Jones went back inside to find the men had forgone dessert at the dining table and were already adjourned to the lounge nibbling on sweet cakes with their drinks. They were discussing the box of cigars and other trophies from exotic voyages. Jones went to the decanter on the cabinet and poured drinks. The Captain was in the highest of moods and hadn't even made mention of Maggie's undignified exit. He seemed to have drawn the conclusion that, as the teacher was a man, she was no longer needed, and she probably lasted longer than he had expected anyway.

Jones passed the glasses. The Captain raised his glass high. "Long live the Queen!" The others echoed in like. They positioned their glasses for a re-fill, and Jones did the honours. Another couple of toasts and the room seemed warmer and friendlier. Jones sipped his subsequent toasts inconspicuously, praying quietly. Tonight was supposed to bring the truth out into the open but the unexpected arrival of Hastings seemed to drive it further underground. Should he let it pass? Should he just come clean?

Then, as if the Captain suddenly remembered the purpose of the event, he congenially pointed to a photographic portrait of Alexander on the wall. "So, Hastings... do you think you could teach a lad like him, get him to become a scholar of note?"

Leon glanced at the frame and saw the likeness immediately. "That's either you or the son of your twin brother!" he declared boldly. The Captain hooted jovially. "And," Hastings continued, "I'm guessing it'd take more skills than I possess, to give him proper book learning."

The Captain paused and tried to focus on his words. "Are you saying my son is an idiot?"

"Oh no!" he said with a laugh. "I'm saying I couldn't teach, even if my life... or his, depended on it." He puffed on his cigar and watched the smoke trail on the breeze coming through the windows. He tapped his head. "Ask me a question and I'll give you the answer. Ask me to *explain* that answer to you..." he shrugged, stumped for an explanation of this personal phenomenon. "Always been that way... never sat well with my tutors. For some reason, they *always* needed a *reason*." He laughed at his witty way with words.

The Captain quietly put down his glass. Jones stepped back warily. "Are you suggesting you'd make a very poor schoolteacher?" the Captain asked, covering his intent with a sweep of his cigar.

"Suggesting?" he scoffed and topped up his glass. "That's subtle! Some things a man does because he's got to; some things he does because he wants to; and some things no fellow should *ever* go near unless he's been called." He waved his cigar at the portrait, leaving a trail of smoke in its wake. "I reckon that is right up there with the priesthood. I haven't got that call – no sir-ee..." His voice faded out and he must have sensed a level of disapproval in the Captain's stance. "I have the greatest regard for those who do though... have the call..." he finished weakly.

The Captain knocked ash from his cigar into his glass on the table thoughtfully. "If teaching is a call, what called you to Henderson's Gap?"

Hastings drained his drink. "Well, the thing is... you don't know until you find out for sure, do you? A man's got to be sure...so I had to be sure... I can't go through a lifetime, not knowing... wondering what might have happened if I came... or didn't come. So, I'm here to be sure... that's for sure!"

"Are you serious?" said the Captain with quiet ice in his voice and dropped his cigar into the glass with a clink. "Are we some sort of social experiment for you? To satisfy whether you are *sure*?"

"Well, I had to do something. You've got to admit, Maggie did look a picture tonight. Where did she go? I should go and say goodnight... just to be sure." He seemed to sway in the flickering candlelight, as he downed the last of his drink.

Jones came over and took the glass from his hand. "Come, Hastings, I think we might excuse ourselves and I'll show you the guest quarters." He guided him towards the door.

The Captain stared at his back. "Jones, where *did* Maggie go?"

"Down to the School House Sir – she has moved into the Teacher's rooms. She has things to prepare, ready to start her classes. Sir, she heard that call." And he left with Hastings before he could see what impact this declaration might have on the Captain.

❧•❧

The Captain donned his oilskin coat and hat and walked down the path. He made his way to the schoolhouse, still half not believing what he heard Jones say. The wet grass dragged at his moleskin trousers and the dim light of the lantern fizzed as fine droplets of rain touched the glass.

He turned down the lantern and sat it behind a tree, and he stood back in the darkness. He saw Maggie moving around against the light behind the privacy screen of lattice that had been fixed along the verandah of her personal rooms. She certainly seemed at home.

The Captain had gone straight to the library and rifled through a pile of paperwork on his desk and found the documents delivered last week by Jones. He turned the pages and there under his signature stood her name, scrolled and elegant: Margaret Jane Louise Wick. No smudges, no apologies. He just hadn't checked. The whole thing happened directly under his nose. What other things had been taken out of his hands because he had been sloppy? It was evident to himself he had not taken this school seriously at all. He took it for granted that it was Jones' project and held no real responsibility for it, even though Henderson personally requested his oversight.

He reread her letter... twice. The words stayed the same, but the details seemed to change into something quite different, with the image of her fair complexion and dark hair. Why had he not considered the quality of the teacher for these children important? It had been an inconvenient detail, something to be checked off. He would nit-pick over the governess for his son, and not even check the name of a teacher for their school? It was a personal reproof. He was better than this. At least he had thought he was. He had never been this sluggish over details, ever.

She opened the lattice door separating her residence from the schoolroom and tipped out a cup over the balcony. She lingered as if remembering something, and quietly slid down and sat on the step. Her head between her hands, she sat quietly in the shadows. The rain paused and the night clouds separated. Moonlight spilt over the gumtrees and shone on the puddles lying in the compressed gravel path. She lifted her head and stared at it mesmerized, tears glistening on her cheeks. She bundled her shawl around her shoulders as a breeze brushed her face.

He moved back behind the tree and quietly retreated. Then, on the impulse of a moment, he turned up the lantern and swung it high. The dim light cast more light and he crunched loudly over some fallen twigs, muttering about the mud. He made his way out into the open and the lantern swinging wide, casting weird shadows against the softness of moonlight.

He saw Maggie quietly swipe at her tears and adjust her night-shawl modestly. He almost regretted his boldness until he saw the frank vulnerability in her eyes. This was the same dazzling face that stunned him as they sat at the dining table, waiting for the door to be answered, singing lyrics to a heart craving music. He dropped his arm low so the circle of light shining from his lantern touched the base of the verandah steps. "Jones said I would find you here. You said you were unwell... I came to check... just to be sure." He cringed at using Hastings words.

She raised her eyes, large from the dim night-light. "I, ahh... I had a bit of a shock."

"Are you okay then? You look upset."

She shrugged. "I am. I was not expecting Leon to come here."

He stepped closer. "I'm gathering my assumption that Hastings was the new schoolteacher was a ludicrous misinterpretation of the circumstances. You know him?"

She nodded. "Yeah. We go back a bit." Then she shrugged. It was over anyway. He might as well know. "Actually, we were... on the verge of being engaged."

McCray paused, absorbing the news. The man had made himself comfortable and shared his port. The scoundrel posed as one familiar and ate his food. McCray swallowed and hid the distaste in his mouth. "He seems a benign enough fellow. Holds his liquor and tells a good story. You could do worse..."

"Romantic advice from the Captain. That's interesting..." She smiled sadly.

"Not advice. Just an observation. And, strictly observationally, it does not seem to be the match made in heaven you were looking for?" As he said it, something skipped in his chest. He stepped over another puddle and stood on the other side of the rough wooden stair. "May I? Sit for a moment?"

She raised her brow in surprise and then nodded. "Funny thing is – I've always thought that romance was something that aligned itself more with Greek Mythology rather than originating in heaven." She laughed cynically. She wasn't far wrong. "For me, romance is like the legend of the Minotaur; a dangerous labyrinth to navigate, that will tear you apart and eat you up in the end." Yes, her Minotaur lived. Her faceless, nameless hero had not yet arrived to save her from being sacrificed. "Leon's okay. We share history. But it's just like you said – benign... bland almost. I don't think I was after *bland*..."

McCray sat still, looking at the moonlight in the puddles. He quietly observed the tightness in his chest again. He didn't want to think about what it might mean. She looked sideways at his silence. "Oh Sir, I am sorry. I should not have said that. He was your guest."

"Well, he wasn't exactly invited. But yes... we talked about a good many things." He paused and looked along the verandah of the schoolhouse, dim and dingy in the moonlight. "So, this is the opportunity that 'far exceeded your expectations'?"

Here it comes... she thought, internally bracing herself. Maggie waited, the silence distending the distance between them, her anxiety rising. Finally, she blurted, "Sir, I know how this must seem, but I so wanted to have the chance to prove myself at this. I just felt you wouldn't consider me. I know you feel justified in the termination of my appointment with Alex, but I would not do *anything* to jeopardize these children. My desire is to sincerely give them what they might otherwise miss. Even the excursion you considered foolhardy; I could re-consider those limitations. I had not wanted such restrictions on their experiences, but if there was no other way! Jones and Olivia have their heart set on this school. They have worked so hard. Please, Sir, I beg you! Allow me some time to prove myself."

He sat there, considering her face in the moonlight. Years of training, coached in presenting the official austere exterior, held him in check. It was an ability at which he excelled. He attributed his accelerated rise in rank with ease, to this one feature of his make-up more than any other. "You think you should stay, even after everything?" And he privately answered his own rueful notion he indulged at the dinner table: *What if Maggie was the teacher coming to dinner and not some stranger knocking at the door?*

She nodded wearily. "Just a chance, like a trial-period. If the children are not improved; if they are not learning their letters and numbers… But Sir, you be the judge based on your assessment of what I do here; not from a retribution of a past account."

Relief rushed to his head. She *intended* to stay. At least for a while. She had not just been waiting for the charmingly bland Hastings to come and sweep her into his arms, and then ride off on his charmingly bland stead back to his mansion in the low hills of civilization. "Well..." he coughed slightly, to recover the equilibrium in his voice, "Our agreement requires regular reviews and progress reports. I would suggest weekly updates, given the circumstances. Friday afternoons at the end of the week would seem appropriate. I will also come to inspect the class. You will not be given notice, and I expect you to carry on as if I am not present."

"Sir, if it would reassure you of my intent in this position, I'll put your name on the roll."

He stood up and turned away from the light. "Goodnight Miss Wick. I trust your appointment as the teacher here is in the best interests of the children of Henderson's Gap." As he walked back to the homestead, he shook his head. He was confident there was more. There always was. Experience taught him that. He resolved to know about this teacher... to know Miss Wick... and her secrets, everything. Just to be sure. He was not going to repeat the offence of omission by neglecting details again.

❧ • ☙

7.

Leon stood against a post of the homestead verandah. He languidly knocked the ash out of his pipe and then casually refilled it from his leather tobacco pouch. Maggie had run away to this? His mind floated with pictures of the successful, talented, social Maggie he knew. Images of her laughing; images of her campaigning her latest project; imagines of her dancing, rowing, riding, reading... ran across his vision, teasing what he saw now. This was not Maggie. This was less than country – this was outback. It was absurd that she could waste away in a place like this.

He stood up tall as he saw her coming through the gate towards the main entrance and he strode out to meet her. "Maggie – good morning! Determined as ever I see, to make me wait on a tight-rope."

Maggie smiled. "Leon, your life is not so narrow and definitely full of more options than a tight rope."

"No, My Beauty, my heart is strung out. I'm walking that line. Why else would I be here?"

Maggie laughed. "Oh, Leon – you are as charming as ever. I'll take the compliment," she shrugged, "but I'm right none the less."

"Are you serious? You think I came all this way without being sincere?"

"I have absolutely no doubt you believe you are sincere," said Maggie.

"And that doesn't touch you? Heartless, heartless woman... shame on you Margaret."

Maggie considered him. "Why are you here Leon?" she asked quietly.

"Oh Maggie, come on – you can't be serious about this?" he indicated the rolling hills beyond the fenced yard. "I know you have memories here, but you have outgrown them. You are gifted and gloriously popular. You will shrivel out here."

"Have you thought to ask *me* why I am here... and for how long?"

"Well, obviously it has developed into more than a family reunion. I know about the governess job Maggie. We discussed this. You don't have to work. Mother is expecting you back, and even Father, with all his righteous objections, has encouraged me in this. Come home with me Maggie."

She looked out into the open spaces beyond him, and quietly considered the freedom she had reached out to hold in her hand. She wanted so much to see if she could ever hold that same music in her heart. "Leon, would you come for a walk with me? I want to show you something."

He hesitated and reluctantly nodded. "Very well." As they followed the track down to the schoolhouse, he restlessly tried to remind her of the good things, the city things, the civilized things she was missing. Maggie hardly heard. She was trying to picture how Leon would react to what she had to show him. Very rarely did she offer Leon an invitation into her dreams. Today she needed to try. Today she would give him the opportunity to see, not just who he thought she was, but something that was genuinely part of herself, and why she needed to stay here for a while. This was not her 'forever-plan' by any stretch of the imagination. But it was for now. It was very much part of her life journey. She nearly had it ripped out from under her and she desperately needed to hold it close for a while. There was nothing quite as effective as believing something is lost, then to make it shine brighter than jasper – uncommon and beautiful. This is what she had accessed; this was her treasure now.

She paused at the clearing around the schoolhouse. Even with its new coat of milk-paint, she knew there was a drab air about it. The quarters, the creaking windmill and rusty water-tank had a used look from years of service for restless, unruly jackaroos. She glanced up at Leon. A distinct look of contempt hovered in his eye. "Don't judge by appearances Leon, there is a substance in this that is very honourable." To his credit, he said nothing. Maggie took him into the classroom, and he sat awkwardly on one of the benches. She showed him the slates Jones had framed in wood and the bookshelf lined with cast-offs from the homestead library. Her desk and chair had been furnished from the guest room.

As she was speaking, he watched her face light with animation, shining with ownership. "Wow. This has really captured you. It is just like you to want to do this for – what... just a dozen kids? That is the Maggie I love... philanthropist, crusader, advocate..."

Maggie paused. "So, you're not displeased with this endeavour?"

"Maggie, come on. How can I be? This is a dream you're living, and a blind man could see you're passionate about it."

"That surprises me."

"Why? I'm seeing you focused and excited again. These are good things, Maggie."

She nodded and smiled softly. "Thank you, Leon."

"It relieves me in a way. Yes. Do this. Get it out of your system, so that when you're done with your missionary experience, you'll be able to come back to Fairfield Estate and settle down."

"I beg your pardon?"

"How long do you think you'll need? One day you *will* wake up from your dream. You know that, don't you?"

"Leon, what if this is not just a missionary experience? What if it is a lifestyle choice I don't wake up from?"

"I would say there can be no logic in a decision that would bury you here indefinitely. That would be way too obsessive, even for you Maggie."

Maggie turned away from him and went and sat down at the desk facing the benches. She sat in this seat so many times... even after dark. She liked the way it felt; she liked the view it would give of the faces in front of her; she liked the sensation of purpose. She absently picked up a volume that sat on the desk and felt the pages under her fingers. Raising her eyes to Leon she looked for any sign he really understood her need to pursue this to the end. And she didn't even know where or when or what the end of this would be.

It was dawning on her as a distinct possibility, that she already knew she would not be going back to the stately home on Fairfield Estate. "I hear you, Leon. I hear you loud and clear. But I want you to hear me as well. I will not like *me* if I don't do this. If I despise myself, I cannot possibly have anything left for those around me, including you. That is not the way to start a betrothal, much less a marriage. I feel you fell in love with a mirage... someone who is not me at all. I've been so lost and disconnected from the things that move me that it seems I can't imagine *not* doing this when I have just found it. Since you can't see me doing this, other than as some sort of transitory phase, I'm struggling to ultimately reconcile that. In this, I will not compromise."

"See Maggie, that is the ridiculous thing. There are plenty of avenues of compromise; dozens of schools around. If this is so urgent – let's get you an appropriate appointment. Mother has contacts. There is a nice little finishing school on the bay. We could have you in there within the week. Done."

She shook her head. So disappointed. He had not heard. "Leon, for the last few years, you have perpetually presented me with avenues of compromise. And I *do* believe in give and take, but have you ever noticed all those appropriate opportunities are constantly on your terms and the 'give' is on my side? *This* is something I have done, my way!"

"Yeah. And look at it, Maggie. It is a pretty poor effort, don't you think?"

She stood up and slammed the book down on the desk. "That is enough Leon! I didn't invite you in here to insult me. Go back to Fairfield Estate. Find someone who will fit your tidy life. There are plenty of others who can make you look good. You don't need me to do that."

He paused and then stood up stoically. There was the suspicion of an ultimatum in his stance. "So, this is your decision? You don't want to be part of Fairfield anymore?"

"Really Leon? Get some perspective! I was not going to marry an address! It was never about Fairfield Estate."

"You have no idea what you are saying! Fairfield is not just an address – it never has been *just* an *address*. It is connection. Connections are powerful allies and formidable foes. Don't underestimate my disappointment, Maggie."

"That smacks of schoolyard bullying. And let me remind you, Leon, I am a teacher who takes a very dim view of bullies. Just leave. It is over... completely over. And when I wake up from my dream, I will be able to say I did it without Fairfield's connections, or your manipulating terms, or my compromise. That will be a first for me, and I like the taste of it."

࿔•࿔

In the silence of the schoolroom, she sat back down at the desk. She placed her head on her arms and silent tears slid down her cheeks. It was no surprise Leon and Fairfield were over. She had known that when she stepped off the stagecoach months ago, so why should she grieve now? Her decision to come to Henderson's Gap was catapulted into action the night Leon had planned to propose. In his confidence he had the whole family leering like classical Greek theatrical masks all through dinner. Missus Hastings began alluding to china patterns and heirloom lace; Mister Hastings started talking about secession plans to the Hastings assets; his twin sisters were giggling and poking and rolling their eyes. It was too overwhelming. So, before the question could be posed she made an announcement of her own. "I've decided to go back to Henderson's Gap for a while. I believe this will give me some time to think about my future and to see my family again. I will be leaving the day after tomorrow."

It was like throwing iced water on a cat. Leon had a tantrum and left; the girls burst into tears; Missus Hastings consoled herself with the fact that although the proposal was never finalized, the servants had prepared an excellent menu. Mister Hastings was the only one who looked relieved.

Now the relief was Maggie's. She had not folded for the convenient. She had not taken the way of least resistance. Yet at the same time, it felt like saying goodbye to an old pair of slippers: familiar and worn, but no longer fitting well. Even if she came to the point where she regretted this moment, just now — it felt fresh to walk around bare-foot. She had increasingly struggled walking in Fairfield shoes. They dictated every step with predictable schedules and lofty expectations.

Commit your way... Maggie closed her eyes and laid her head on the book lying on the desk. "Oh, God..." It was more of a groan than a prayer. "I just did something even I recognize as very delusional. I told the handsome heir of a fortune that I would prefer to live in three rooms on a provisional teacher's salary. But regardless of whether it really is delusional or not,

God, I believe you understand this desire in me to walk with resolve and to make an impact. You have given me a gift here, suddenly and unexpectedly. I want to make a difference. Help me to do well in this school. Help me not to look back and turn into salt."

She wiped her eyes and sat up. Her gaze fell on the book that lay on her desk, and she picked it up curiously. It was a book of Greek mythology. Funny. How pertinent, as she was just thinking of those Greek histrionic masks. Yes, it was time to take off her own theatrical mask. She had been as guilty as any in that circle of only presenting the character they wanted her to play. She opened the cover. The frontispiece was a classical line drawing of Minotaur being challenged by Theseus. Maggie stared at the illustrated plate for a long time, the bull's nostrils flaring and snorting angrily. She knew she had handled it poorly, just running away from the Hastings Empire without so much as an explanation. But she felt trapped. Here she had started to gain a sense of what was under the mask. Exactly what that was, she hardly knew. Was it time to challenge her Minotaur? She didn't think so. Not yet. The sacrifice of Leon was a tragedy perhaps, but he was no match for this monster. In her heart, she believed that.

8.

Maggie stood on the verandah and shook hands with parents. The kids buzzed, calling and chasing and pulling pigtails that had been laboriously plaited for the first day of school. She recorded the last of the enrolment details and parents said their goodbyes. The children hardly batted an eyelid.

Maggie suddenly realized there was no school bell. She looked at the children playing and was not sure how to assemble them. She tried clapping her hands, waving them in, calling to them... but the current game of kick-the-tin was not to be interrupted. Maggie felt her pulse rate rising. If she couldn't marshal the kids into class, would she ever be able to instil facts and knowledge? In desperation, she stuck her thumb and forefinger in between her teeth and let an ear-piercing whistle split through the schoolyard antics. Every child came to a screaming halt, and rallied into line, with a look of awe showing in Tom's eyes.

She ushered them into the classroom and arranged them according to age along the benches: boys on one side; girls on the other; youngest at the front. She looked at the details on the page in front of her and took her first roll call: "Ladies, please stand as I call out your name: Priscilla, Wilma, Jemimah, Patsy, Keziah, Pauline, and little Keren. Yes, well done. You may be seated. Boys? Andy, Tom, Gerard… Gerard, please stand. Thank you. Karl and Peter."

It was a landmark moment. A mountain had been conquered, and with that, her confidence grew. She had spent so much time in thinking and planning and working out how to approach this day of firsts: first opening, first lessons, first interactions. She had each child stand and give an introduction. She handed out the slates and they started writing alphabet letters. She chose a book from the bookshelf and began reading a story, opening up the door to a world of wild, adventurous literature.

She looked up to see the Captain standing quietly in the back of the classroom. She coloured slightly as she remembered his dictum – inspection: any day, any time. She was irritated. Could he not extend faith for at least her first day? He was not going to take this away from her. He would have no cause. Her story rose with suspense and drama, the characters leapt out of the pages, and then slowly and gently she rounded them up and put them back inside the covers at the end of a chapter and closed the book. They groaned and wanted her to continue.

She stood. "Students: we have a visitor. Please stand and say good morning to Captain McCray." They mumbled a greeting, then she dismissed the students for break. "Ladies first. We will resume class on the hour. Gentlemen, courtesy please: wait for the ladies to leave the room. No talking." She walked to the back of the classroom as the last boy left the room sedately and battle-charged out into the yard. "So, Mister McCray. How are your impressions of school this morning?"

He looked startled by the directness of her address. Captain for the students; Mister for him. He had considered what to say as he watched her reading, drawing the students in with the expressions and lilts of a master storyteller. Who would know she had never taught in a school before? "You ahh... you have created a fine sense of order."

"Oh. I was hoping for something more in the line of fertile minds being challenged," she said. He was really very annoying. How typical of a solider to only value discipline. Granted it was a significant part, but not the only part.

He cringed inside. He had hoped to compliment her, to encourage her efforts. Yet it seemed no matter what he said, it was not the right thing. His mind went blank. He nodded and turned to leave. He stopped at the door briefly. "Come to the library this afternoon after class. Bring with you a list of the things you have found wanting. I need your requirements considered as we develop the forward planning submission for the Board of General Education. Make it as comprehensive as you can."

She gazed after him as he strode down the stairs to his horse, mounted and rode off. His abruptness left a sting in her throat. She shook her head. What sort of list? More books? A holding yard for the ponies the kids rode to school? Was that too much? When he was talking about forward planning – was it two months or ten years? She didn't want to strain an already stretched relationship, but he *did* say comprehensive. She guessed this list-exercise was probably meaningless and academic, but if she put absolutely everything on it, then she might return some of the irritation she felt from his quarter. And he could never say he had not been given the information. Then they would really see who had *the best interests* of the children at heart. She walked outside and sat down on a bench under the trees, watching the children inspect their lunch pails and down stale sandwiches and biscuits before they brought out the tin to continue to play their interrupted game.

She knew that what these children already had far exceeded some of their counterparts in other regional schools. Provisional schools, especially those privately sponsored by local working communities were notoriously under-resourced. Once it became known they were opening a school, stories came out of the wood-work of canvas-tent classrooms; water running through improvised classrooms during the wet season; classes jammed in the cold corners of worker's sheds while men came in and out to cook their lunches over the stoves. Perhaps they were reassuring themselves that this little schoolhouse was okay, even in its worn state of shabbiness.

If this were an established school, what would it look like? Colour – she craved colour. She could use some of the old tea-chests in the shed and pull apart the sides to create posters with leftover milk paint from the renovation. Sammy would help her hang them. They would have a garden, turning the soil-bed with tools from the main house, and the children could maintain it with digging sticks. A library, readers, writing pens, inkwells on each desk...

The lunch hour was over, and she was assembling the students again for their afternoon session to start their number drills and scripture lesson. When she dismissed the students at the end of the afternoon, she sat at her desk in the stillness of the empty room and took a deep breath. Wow. First day. Eventually, she opened her drawer and retrieved those first sheets of paper where she had allowed herself to dream. She picked up her pen, dipped it in the inkwell and started to write. Her thoughts flowed onto the paper. If he wanted a comprehensive list – she could give him that. She jotted down the things she would need for projects of all sizes. As she wrote, she realized this was a valuable foray into the realm of possibility – just like that very first night, one she determined to visit again, and again. Her garden was mapped out, the types of posters drafted. A very quiet smile broke across her face. The ground had been turned.

༺ • ༻

Maggie knocked on the library door and waited with the list in her hand. Why did she have to come here waving a white flag? The man behind the desk was her adversary. She resented his pompous attempts to be attentive, and his diligent efforts to present himself as conscientious. The words he said in the dark on Saturday night echoed again in her mind: "I trust your appointment is in the best interests of the children of Henderson's Gap." What did he care about the *best interests* of those under his jurisdiction? He didn't even have the energy to work out who the teacher of the school really was. She sceptically considered that a man of his rank and experience could do better than farming unless there had been some demotion of shame. She was sure he could not be here just because of the fine conditions and excellent pay that Henderson offered.

She went to knock impatiently again when the panel door opened. He looked at her suspended there like a bird snap-frozen mid-flight. She quickly lowered her arm, as he stepped back nodding a greeting. She coloured slightly as she walked through the doorway, the tension in her chest making her hands tremble slightly. How annoying! He must never know. He must never have any inkling that his closeness unsettled her so.

Rather than returning to his desk, McCray moved over towards the chesterfield lounge by the bookshelves and offered her a seat. She sat slowly, wondering. He did not sit behind his attitude and rank, or stand astride as if on parade, but leaned thoughtfully against the mantle. "How did you find your first day? Were there many things overlooked in our preparation for you?"

She swallowed. "Given there was apparently not the slightest notion I was privileged in achieving this appointment, I hardly think preparations were solely for my benefit. A school's purpose is for the children after all." She saw he considered her remark and noticed the grim line of his mouth.

He swallowed and cleared his throat. "I feel I owe you an apology. I allowed some matters that were my responsibility to go unattended. I have resolved to attend to these things in the future."

She looked at him keenly, but he said nothing further. Well then. One confession deserves another. "Acknowledging my inexperience and the frantic preparations made in such a short time frame, I feel we fared reasonably well. I have compiled the list you requested. I was uncertain of your expectations, so I have grouped them into immediate, short-term and long-term..." She opened the sheet of paper and passed it over.

He looked at it but did not move to take it. "Please read it and explain each item as you go." Maggie raised her eyebrows and studied his face. He met her eyes easily and casually commented. "It will give me an understanding of what's behind the requests. If the longevity of the school is our goal, these things need to be considered to make a plan going forward." And, he added quietly in his mind, *I will not make the same mistake twice: details will not be overlooked. Nor will I need to carry the conversation if you do the talking.*

"Okay..." She swallowed. This was awkward. Suddenly it became personal. She had merely expected to hand over the list and escape. Instead, it looked like it was going to be a drawn-out, torturous affair, more than likely with her hopes for the school being dissected and invalidated, yet again, as 'a pretty poor effort'.

She cleared her throat. "I'm sorry – would you mind if I had a glass of water?" She put the paper on the lounge and started to rise.

He quickly went to his desk and poured a glass from the tray covered in starched linen. As he handed her the glass he said, "My apologies... again. I should have ordered tea. I'll go and see if Lonnie can do something."

As he left the room Maggie groaned and covered her eyes. What was he doing? It was totally perplexing and yet, in all honesty, he had not said or done anything inappropriate. It was just that... it was unexpected. Even with all the pep-talks she had given herself on the walk up to the house, bracing herself as she waited at the door, she now felt totally unprepared. Every time she met him, something changed. Every time. Not once had he done the same thing in the same way. The man was as unpredictable as a cricket in a frying pan. Where was the regimented soldier's routine?

He came back and offered to top up her glass of water. "Lonnie will be here shortly. I'll guarantee she won't be long. She is curious to see how you fared on your first day."

Maggie blinked. She had not heard him acknowledge their relationship before. She wondered what he really thought about that. She fully expected their cross-cultural family would be a problem for a man of position. Certainly, Lonnie had never warmed to him. He rose when Lonnie came into the room. Lonnie looked sideways at Maggie and saw a frown knitted tightly across her brow.

Maggie barely spoke above a whisper, her nerves stretched from tiredness, compounded by the tension she felt from this interview. "Thank you, Lou Mou, you are kind. It has been a big day."

"Come when you are done... and tell Lou Mou about it." She said something in Mandarin as she put the tea-tray on the small table near the lounge. Maggie smiled and quietly responded in Mandarin as she reached for her cup.

"I will – we shouldn't be long." She took a sip and felt herself unwind as she inhaled the familiar aromas of the infusion. It was like a memory she suddenly could relax into. She sometimes wondered what other things Lonnie added to her tealeaves.

McCray watched Lonnie leave and then poured himself a cup of tea. He said nothing for quite a while. Then he motioned stiffly to Maggie's list. "So, what was the first thing that caught your attention?"

He may be a lot of things, but she had to reluctantly acknowledge an element of humanity etched into this request, however undeveloped that quality may be. Maggie thought it was something she could play to. What if he could see and experience the school through her eyes? She quietly vowed to slowly draw back the curtain to let him picture it from her perspective. She was a storyteller; she could do this. So, she shrugged and laughed. "That's easy – a school bell. I'm very disappointed in myself that the thing at the top of my list is something as mundane and practical as a bell. However, I am now *totally* convinced it is an indispensable item in a schoolteachers' suite of tools. First thing this morning I was in the rather challenging situation of looking at a dozen children scattered in every possible direction, engrossed in the most epic battle of kick-the-tin, and trying to get their attention for roll call. It meant resorting to a most undignified whistle, although the boys were visibly impressed."

"Muster Roll: the drill sets the tone of every day."

"And much easier with a bell. Anything has got to be an improvement on whistling at them like cattle dogs." She laughed at the ridiculous moment and sipped her tea. It dawned on her she may have said too much. She dared to look at him over the rim of her cup.

McCray didn't bat an eyelid. "Yes, preserving the decorum of our schoolteacher must always be a priority. Next?"

Maggie went through the list. He would ask an occasional question or invite a comment to clarify. Maggie found herself talking freely, eager to instil an appreciation of what she saw. If he could acknowledge the picture, she had more chance he would not obstruct her ambition of making this school as equitable as any vested establishment. Finally, she paused and confessed, "That's all I had."

McCray's expression didn't change. "Anything you've thought of since we have been talking? Additional items you want to add?" He waited as she shook her head. "There you go Miss Wick, not so daunting being brought before the school committee?"

Maggie looked a little shocked and searched his dark grey eyes, "far less intimidating than I expected.

Thank you." She rose to go. "Is there anything else you require of me, Sir?"

"Probably, but that's a good start. I believe Lonnie will be beside herself if you don't alleviate her pain soon. I feel like I have been locked inside a cage with a growling Chinese Tiger all day."

Maggie paused and frowned quizzically, then shook her head with a smile. "Yes. She is formidable when she's pacing. I'd better go..."

McCray watched her leave without moving, and then drained his tea. He went back to work at his desk with a pensive furrow on his brow.

♊•♊

Maggie found Lonnie wringing her hands in the kitchen. She opened the door and quietly went and gave her a hug. Lonnie in seconds had poured another cup of tea. "Lou Mou, you were quite right. I felt more like Daniel being thrown into the lions' den than attending a school meeting."

Lonnie grinned mischievously. "The angels shut their mouths."

"That is one way to explain how I survived an interview with the formidable Mr McCray."

Lonnie arched her dark brow. "You mean Captain?"

"Lou Mou, everyone around here may call him Captain, the children will even refer to him as Captain, but he is *not* captain to me. He is no longer commissioned in the Queen's army, and as far as I am concerned this artificial use of rank is unimpressive. I am not going to call him "Captain". I can guarantee you; he will not get it from me – ever!"

Lonnie grinned. "You had a good day Missy!" She tapped her china cup with her finger as if making an announcement. "It's like what Sammy says when you were little: good days you spark; bad days you bark. Today I glad you spark. Were the children very good?"

Maggie sipped her tea, smiling. "The children were too scared to do anything today. Tomorrow we will see their true colours." She nibbled on a slice of bran-loaf. "Or perhaps today I was too scared, and tomorrow they will see *my* true colours."

಄•಄

When Maggie opened up the classroom the next morning, a tin whistle dangled from the doorknob. She unravelled the red cord curiously and held it tightly in her hand. It infused her with courage and she quietly thanked the guardian who came to her rescue with such a simple solution. This was so like Jones. She had bumped into him walking home from her meeting and they had laughed about the kick-the-tin saga. In many respects, his role in her life had not changed. Hadn't he offered her this opportunity after all? She smiled at the thought that his lips had also touched this mouthpiece, and lifted it to her lips, tentatively testing the shrill note. She wondered if she had yet outgrown her childish infatuation. It seemed Minotaur lived on. Perhaps the only way left to acknowledge her regard for him was to be the best teacher his kids would ever have. She opened the door and arranged her books on her desk. She placed the whistle next to her inkwell and nibs. It rolled forward and she reached out to stop it. As she lifted her fingers, she saw an inscription faded and worn engraved on the stem. She looked at it intrigued, and then dropped it like it was hot. The scrolled letters were D McC.

9.

Maggie opened her eyes, stretched her arms above her pillow and smiled. Blinko purred on the foot of her bed in agreement. The sun was not yet up. The tranquil darkness was fading, and the morning star was bright on the horizon. Everything was perfect. She pulled on her boots and jacket and made her way to the river. The waterway bordering Aunt Winifred's garden welcomed her many early mornings like this. They had an uncommon friendship, the river and her. They often talked together over the hush of the water lapping the hull and the oars dipping through the ripples of glass.

The old boatshed held the remnants of a bygone era – evidence of a fleeting romance old Misses Henderson had with elegant river parties amid umbrellas, baskets and cane picnic chairs. Some debris from rising flood levels poked through the lattice and fretwork. Now it was used for the storage of practical items like fishing tackle and fencing shovels, stacked in beside neglected rowboats. All of them needed major work to be water-worthy, except for one small dinghy, and Maggie had easily prepared it for this moment.

She slid the boat down the bank and pushed out into the water. Maggie loved that sound of the water rustling against the oars in the calm quiet of the pre-dawn morning. She was soon absorbed in the motion of rowing, the bow slicing through the quiet mist rising from the water as a peaceful chorus of birds sang their morning psalms to their Creator. She saw a trail of bubbles as a pair of platypuses played and tussled, then duck-dived away from sight. A wedge-tailed eagle swept low over the water and maneuvered with elegant grace through the arch of trees to a tall gum to stand sentry. Water-dragons stood motionless and mute blending into the wood by the bank – their eyes alert and their throats pulsating, ready to drum out a call. The startling azure blue of a kingfisher darted into the water now reflecting the morning sky streaked with pink and lemon. Every sight was a leap of worship in her heart – acknowledging uncommon beauty and harmony… and her place in it. Yes, it had been too long… too long indeed.

Reluctantly she turned the boat home. She felt refreshed and her head clear, like rain-washed air. Knowing she had class this morning seemed to confirm that her teaching position was as harmonious as the river at dawn – it fitted the rhythm of her life… and life at Henderson's Gap. She stepped onto the shore and her boot slipped in the mud. She grabbed the side of the boat for balance and regained her footing.

"You should be careful Ma'am."

She turned around startled. "Mister Casey. Well, good morning."

"Mornin'..." He eyed her as she struggled with the boat.

She paused, uncomfortable with his surveillance. "Mister Casey, how is Gerard enjoying school?" She slipped again and reached out to steady herself.

"Like I was saying, you should be careful Ma'am."

"Your concern is appreciated Mister Casey," she said. She noticed his disgruntled tone and where he stood: over her, up on the bank. Maggie looked at his rough countenance. She didn't understand what he was getting at.

"I'm thinking that a little boat like that could just get swept away. Just swept away..." he said again, "...like that schoolhouse of yours. It ain't a done deal... that schoolhouse. My kid can't be expected to learn the way it is. It is an a-atrophy."

She was surprised by his metaphor. The idea seemed a little abstract for his type. His face was smug, possibly because he thought he had been clever. She didn't flinch. "If you feel Gerard's schooling is someway inadequate, or that I am not committed to his education, please... you are free to tell me the reason for your disappointment Mister Casey."

There had been no need to invite him to explain because she could tell he was intent on airing his grievance. He came straight to the point. "The school ain't natural. Them Jones' girls are too old for school. Never heard any of them types needing school past grade three. Any good Christian knows that."

"Being a good Christian seems important to you, Mister Casey." She looked around. There was nowhere for her to go without being directly in his path unless of course, she got back into the boat.

"Damn right. And this ain't right! Them girls should be keepin' house. Anyways, them got no right learning books alongside my boy."

"Mister Casey – you can hardly expect me to agree. The opportunity for me to help your son with his learning would never have come about if someone insisted, I do housekeeping *just* because it is what my parents do. Although of course there is nothing wrong with housekeeping if that is the ambition one chooses." To her, it was about choices.

He swallowed – his straggly beard twitching uncontrollably. This woman would challenge him? His eyes flashed with a creepy antagonism. "It ain't right. Oh, it is all gunna give way all right – and ya gunna get mud all over your pretty little schoolteacher face. Someone proper should be schooling my boy!"

"By 'proper' I assume you mean a man. Well, you could always write an application. I'm sure Captain McCray would consider interviewing anyone who has an interest in the position. He has very high expectations and is always looking to find avenues to improve."

Casey's lip curled in an ugly snarl. He completely understood she was taking the mickey out of him. He had not been able to sign his name on Gerard's enrolment form. He muttered a volley of oaths and his complexion went a shade darker. "You! You think you're better than us Christian folk. But you ain't no better than them types you teach! You being raised by a slinty-eyed Chink! You've got nothing to…"

"Casey! Today is a school morning. Don't detain our schoolteacher any longer."

He spun around and saw McCray on his horse, staring at him with eyes like flint, his mouth firm, and his hand significantly on the butt of his rifle in its leather-case hanging beside his saddle. Casey muttered another string of oaths and strode off in direction of the yards. McCray dismounted and walked down the slope of the bank towards the boat.

Maggie turned away, looking over the river in silence. The harmony of the morning suddenly sounded discordant in her ears. How could something so sweet, abruptly taste so bitter? She looked up into the sky at a gathering bank of clouds, and quickly took a short breath. Emerging from the clouds was the dark head of the Minotaur: surly, incensed and voracious; his appetite insatiable; his presence ominous.

"Miss Wick? Are you okay?" His voice was subdued, washing gently against her rattled nerves like lapping water.

"I... I think so..." She wiped her palms on her skirt and he noticed they trembled.

"I take it you won't be going out for a row this morning." He sounded pleased, like he had saved her on both accounts.

"Actually, I was about to return the boat to the shed, but the bank has been cut away... getting up is a little more arduous than down." She cringed. It sounded like she was begging for help.

He paused and looked at the hull of the boat, noticing it was wet, and then over the river, still and silent in the morning light. "You've already been out this morning? Alone?" It wasn't really a question.

She didn't deny it. "Everything was perfect until I was accosted by that miserable minded parent. It was evident he sought me out."

"Miss Wick, there are under-currents here that are becoming quite turbulent."

What was the panic that surrounded this river? She sighed and turned back towards him. "I would have to disagree. It was absolutely serene on the water this morning."

"I was not talking about the river."

"Is it so wrong to believe in beauty? It *is* possible to appreciate what others find threatening."

"It is naïve to think, Miss Wick, that beauty cannot be dangerous." He looked at her eyes firing up with emotion and wondered if he really understood the truth of that claim. If that was so, he might be placing himself in a great deal of peril. "This place is just like a river – quiet on the surface..." He didn't finish the sentence but was silent for a moment. Then he turned to her. "I heard you recommend Casey apply for your job. The idea has me quite bemused that you would suggest he might be an improvement."

Her neck flushed and she adjusted her scarf discreetly. "I merely said you are always looking to improve, which is true. I have no fear he could satisfactorily write such an application."

"Miss Wick?" She turned around; he stood beside the boat ready to lift. His expression was grim again. "I am encouraging caution. Let someone know when you are down here. Take someone with you."

The colour rose from Maggie's neck unashamedly into her face. Was she a child? The whole point of her morning outings was solitude. "I can't do 'alone' with an entourage. Besides, who do you think would come?" It was preposterous. She was quite capable of handling a boat by herself; except as she tugged on the boat against the cut-out bank it was evident, she could not do it with ease. "You just want to hog-tie me again. No one is in a position to wet-nurse me. And even if they were, it is unreasonable to ask it of them !"

He considered her accusation and it felt like the nuisance of a pesky horsefly that he didn't want to land because he knew it would bite. "Hog-tie would be easier. But I am not one to identify a problem and not be part of the solution. Okay then. Sunday morning."

"Sunday... what?" she said sceptically. He nodded and she realized what he was offering. "No! I'm not going to have you imposing on my river time." It was out before she realized. She quietly applauded herself as she recognized she was not stepping around this man in fear and reverence like so many others. He was just a person, not a frightening austere authority figure... however arrogant he may be.

He quietly looked at her fearless expression of irritation and he found her independence drawing him in. He took a deep breath. Yet this wasn't about independence, but safety. He had responsibilities. She had made him very aware of that. "I'm mindful that as your employer, your safety is my responsibility. Either you find someone to accompany you, or I will be compelled to have the boatshed locked and its contents made inaccessible."

She looked at him and realized he really would impose sanctions on her discovery if it wasn't done his way. She had felt so elated when she found this little boat in the boatshed that no one had used or wanted for a very long time. She could feel it slipping away. Perhaps Casey was right. It could just disappear. When she spoke, her voice was clipped. "Very well.

Just before dawn… five-thirty. And don't talk; I won't say anything – at all."

At that, he could not resist a smile. "Then it won't be all bad." He picked up the boat and carried it up the bank, leaving her standing there.

❧•❧

When Maggie woke up on Sunday morning her arms felt like lead. It was tempting not to go, but she had a point to prove – that the river was important to her, regardless of these ridiculous parameters being imposed. She knew it was not her boat, nor her river. It seemed that if she wanted to experience this, it must be on these terms. The air was chill and she layered her clothing as unattractively as possible. She tied on her headscarf, donned overcoat and boots, and walked to the boat shed.

McCray was already with the boat, down by the water. She nodded to him curtly. He went to offer a greeting, but she held up her hand, and he obediently remained silent. She scrambled into the boat, ignoring his offered hand for support. He shrugged and followed mutely, as she took up an oar.

Maggie was determined not to notice he was there, but she could feel him behind her, and the sound of another oar, slightly out of sync, messed with her rhythm. Her body was in turmoil; her head spun with frustration and her pulse raced. She felt overdressed and peeled off her scarf, and then her overcoat. She didn't notice the reflections on the water or the birds skimming over the surface catching insects in the morning light. A turtle splashed into the water and she jumped. Everything was on edge. This was *not* how morning rowing was supposed to be. It was pointless to try to continue. She was annoyed he had ruined it for her, and she turned the boat around to go back.

When they docked, she jumped out, busily hustling the boat out of the water. McCray stood back and considered her industry. Finally, he said, "I don't get it. What about that is important to you? You didn't enjoy it at all."

She glared at him. "How would you know whether I enjoyed it or not? You cannot read my mind!"

"Believe me your silence says a whole lot: hunched, unyielding posture – stiff as a board. Your rhythm was erratic and your stroke uneven."

"I'm not in training. It was just a morning excursion."

He shrugged. "Just as well – on both accounts. No one would win a championship like that."

It was enough for her to look at him curiously. "Do you know rowing Mr McCray?"

He shrugged. "When I was younger: in another life. But I have no hankering to go to any lengths to revive the experience."

"Meaning?"

"Meaning – it is obvious the excursion has a measure of awkwardness for you and given the circumstances I can't imagine that you will want to do it again."

It sounded like Leon. Another condescending male who felt she needed to get things out of her system. "Then your imagination needs some improvement. You want it to be awkward. But of course, you are relieved of any obligation you feel to attend me."

"The obligation I feel is not dependent on your permission, but on my sense of responsibility. So, if you intend to go through that again, you will let me know and I will be here: awkward and all."

Maggie rolled her eyes. Really, why would he be bothered? "I don't think I would want to inconvenience you so greatly."

"When are you coming back?" He could tell she had stubbornly decided to do so.

"I might not…"

"Well Miss Wick, let's see if your next excursion will be a little more agreeable."

"I doubt it," said Maggie, as they picked up the boat together, and lifted it back to the shed.

కొ•ఆ

10.

Tom was late. Again. He walked boldly up to Maggie's desk and placed a box in front of her. Stepping back, he looked down at his bare feet. *Like father, like son*, thought Maggie. Well, that was a good thing she supposed; his father was Jones. Maggie frowned. Time was a struggle when it came to this family. It was like they had their own internal clock, and no amount of winding the fob-watch she wore as a pendant around her detachable collar could change that. She despaired of being able to instil the sense of responsibility she desired. She waited for some sort of explanation, that perhaps the box was intended as an apology for tardiness, but none came.

Maggie sighed impatiently as Tom averted his gaze. Where was the young man who played Shadows out in the paddock? He couldn't meet her scrutiny and stared at his feet; it seemed less about ordering his ways and more about guilt. His sisters had the same tendency. She had served an embarrassing series of punishments on them, which Priscilla and Jemimah bore in stoic silence. Tom less so. It made no difference.

Maggie called Priscilla over. Perhaps his sister could get through to him where she failed. With no preamble, she laid the situation and the consequences out on the table. "Priscilla, Tom has been tardy again." Maggie paused. "He will have to stand in the corner for this lesson." It felt unusual, talking as if Tom was invisible. She glanced up at the other kids. Gerard was staring at them with a smirk on his face; openly enjoying that Tom had been busted. Maggie noted his delight silently.

Priscilla spoke quietly to Tom and he went to the corner, his eyes bright. She came over to Maggie and leant in so only she could hear. "Tom wanted you to see some of the things he has learnt from the bush." She pointed to the box. "He found this, and wanted to give it to the school because the school has given so much to him."

Maggie regarded her wide-open brown eyes. There was no hint of disrespect or impudence. She checked herself as she heard Gerard mutter something about Tom being the teacher's pet, and other bodily functions that may have contributed to this status. She took a deep breath and decided to risk it. "Priscilla, tell Tom I am honoured." Maggie spoke louder, "As it is a gift to the school perhaps the whole class could come and see what it is?"

Priscilla nodded, and Tom could contain himself no longer. He bounced back to her desk. "I found it this morning Miss Maggie. It was way over by the boundary track. Open it!" The class clambered out of their benches and gathered around her desk, curiosity overtaking their disdain for the moment. She cautiously lifted the lid.

Inside was a bald, gangly baby bird with a generous beak, blinking up at her through bluish lids. It had a broken wing and it was the ugliest thing Maggie had ever seen. "Will it live?" she asked sceptically.

Tom's hands quickly reach in and lifted it out. "Dunno. Dad says cockatoos will be loyal as any dog if you get them young and treat them nice. It fell out of a tree, so it's probably gunna die. Figured we gotta try."

She looked around at the wide-eyed faces peering into the box. "Anybody here an expert on parrots?" A bank of blank looks stared back at her. "I think this means we have a lot to learn." It immediately materialized into a school project. She asked what they thought they might need to know and who might be able to help them with information. Then she asked, "Tom, have you named him yet?" The class offered their ideas and Maggie wrote them down: Cocky, Sid, Monster, Scamp, Bozo and Twinkle from little Keren. They had some discussion without agreement. His good looks certainly had a prehistoric edge. Monster was not too far from the truth. They laughed when Maggie leafed through a natural history book and showed the class what a pterodactyl, the historical bird, may have looked like. The final vote was for, Pterodactyl: "Terry" for short. Gerard was so proud that his cynical suggestion led to the final naming. It immediately gave him a level of guardianship for the featherless juvenile.

As an acknowledgment of his contribution, Maggie paired Gerard with Tom to take responsibility for the bird after school. The girls would design and knit a couple of jackets to keep him warm until his feather's matured. The boys were to build a perch on the verandah and a portable cage to carry him in. Each student was to research some of the things they needed to know. They were to ask anyone they knew who might be able to provide good advice about looking after birds, and then they would compile their own 'Caring for Terry' manual.

"Can I see you, Tom?" Maggie said as the kids bolted for the door at home time. He hesitated as he held Terry's box and then shoved it over to Gerard's care. Tom stood, still glowing from the success of his gift. "Thank you for rescuing Terry," Maggie started. "He will make a great school pet." She paused and looked at her hands. "Tom, I still have the issue of you being late for class so many times." He looked at his feet and said nothing. "Tom, if you are late tomorrow, I will keep you back after school to make up the time you miss in the morning. Do you understand?" He bit his lip and nodded mutely.

Maggie thought his eyes shone too brightly and thought maybe he regarded the whole thing a joke.

As Sammy walked her back to the teacher's quarters that night it was like the planets had aligned and life for the moment was again perfectly in place. Maggie slipped on her house scuffs with an air of deep satisfaction. She sat for a while looking at the stars from the front step. She thought over the morning. It could have gone any number of ways. The fact she had won class unity on an interesting project made her smile. Even Gerard had whooped with satisfaction as he had taken Terry's box from Tom's hand. Perhaps she was good at this after all. Perhaps this was something she could do... and do well. Perhaps it really wasn't a "pretty poor effort" after all. Snub to you Leon, she thought triumphantly.

Tom wasn't at school the next day; neither was Priscilla, or little brother Andy. His sisters just shrugged when Maggie asked questions. Gerard at least was happy to have the kudos of being Terry's uncontested custodian.

After classes, Maggie tidied up and spent some time completing some lesson preparation; then she went up to the Jones' cottage. Jemimah stood at the gate with her dark eyes staring innocently at Miss Maggie, her foot determinedly jamming the hinge from opening. "Dad's still out at the paddocks. He won't be back until sundown. You could come back then if it's important."

"I actually came to speak with your mother."

"She says it's best if you talk with Dad."

Maggie raised her eyebrows. She had not expected that of Olivia. But then Maggie realized that Jones had been around every time they had spoken. For Maggie and her independent way, she thought Olivia's reliance on her husband was a little weak.

Maggie came back when the light was fading. Jones welcomed her to the outside hearth, and they sat on logs positioned as forms around the fireplace. Jones offered her a cup of tea, which Jemimah wordlessly poured. She was cooking dinner and the other girls fussed over their Dad. Jones sat down opposite her, crossing his legs out in front of him. "The girls told me you came earlier. Sorry for the bother but Liv is not here."

"She's left you?" The words sprang from her mouth before she could stop them. Her mind raced.

There was a twist of humour around his mouth. "Well of course – if she's away... but she'll be back."

"Oh." It sounded like Olivia had popped down to the bakery to buy a loaf of bread. "Should I wait? How long will she be?" Of course, Henderson's Gap didn't have a bakery, and the nearest town was three hours ride.

He considered her for a moment, fun flickering in his eyes. And then, as if he thought the better of it, quietly said, "That would usually be about a week, sometimes longer."

"Usually?" Did she abandon her husband often? He seemed curiously comfortable with the idea. "A week?" The girls giggled.

Jones smiled like he had the most fantastic secret. "Yep. She's gone walkabout."

Maggie swallowed. That Olivia was part aboriginal was uncontested. That she would still want to engage in their custom, seemed odd. After all, she married a Christian man. "Can she do that? I mean she has a Christian faith. Isn't that, a... well, like a... tribal... pagan thing to do?"

Jones looked at his boots. "She's gone to visit her family. Tom, Andy and Priscilla have gone with her."

"She's taken the children? What about school?" Maggie felt scandalized. She could not understand Jones and Olivia's relationship.

Jones looked up at her and considered her quietly. "You feel it is not appropriate the children visit their grandparents?"

"Well sure if they were just going to have tea, but isn't Walkabout like a spiritual, heathen thing? How can you condone that?"

Jones shifted his weight and took the enamel plate Jemimah offered him. He pointed his fork at the stew. "Want to join us for dinner?" Maggie felt like she was ten years old again, sitting by the fireside waiting for Jones to teach her something. She didn't eat at the big-house every night. She had taken some fruit and a packed supper tonight because she wasn't sure how long or short this visit might be.

She nodded. "Sure." Keziah and Keren giggled again and sat down, one on each side of her with their bowls. Jemimah scooped out another plate and offered it to her. She sat beside her father, the similarity of his features with her dark adolescent complexion giving her a striking look. They said grace.

Jones scooped up some stew and commended Jemimah on her efforts. Then he returned to their conversation as if there had hardly been a pause. "It seems I have come to understand *Walkabout* as code – a thing to tell the white-fellas because we are not so good at understanding what these things mean to them."

"What things?"

"Things like the land, family, the bush... their ways. Liv is very loyal – to her family, and to me. She does an extraordinary job balancing those two dimensions in her hand. There are the obligations in this white-way, and there is the pull of her-way. She needs to go and appreciate the land and her connection there every so often. It is her place. She says she cannot ignore it."

He took another fork-full of hearty stew. When he finished his meal, he asked for a second round. Jemimah served him another liberal helping.

"What is interesting to me though is the idea of the Kingdom of God – how it stands like neutral ground between the two. It is loyal to no-one but itself. It doesn't endorse one way over the other. Some things about white-fella-way are like Kingdom culture, most of it isn't. Some things about their way is Kingdom-minded too, like being custodians of the land – not just using it up and moving on. That's a commission that goes back to the Garden of Eden. But I have to remember ultimately, I am a Kingdom citizen. When I look at it this way, it helps me understand I have the liberty to visit and engage with either side... but I cannot stay there. It is like I have a neutral armistice that I carry around with me. That is the way Jesus walked. He didn't stand in the Roman camp or in the Hebrew camp of the Religious Jews. He walked the Kingdom way... straight on through... sometimes alone."

Maggie stared into the coals. There was a peace and acceptance in what he said. They sat for a while, each with their own thoughts. Maggie smiled to herself. It was just like Jones to go far deeper than she intended. Really, she had just wanted to see if he could reinforce the importance of the children getting to school on time. Now that would sound petty to bring it up. His reflective smile suggested to Maggie it was not a simple situation, so their response to it could not be simple. She put down her plate and thanked the girls for their hospitality. Jones stood and wiped his hands on his moleskins. "Thanks, Maggie, for the school. The kids are really getting on. I am so proud of them. It's just that, for these kids," his hand swept across to where the girls sat by the fire poking the coals with a stick, "they have two schools to attend. Not many people get that."

11.

Maggie refused to inform Mr McCray of her intention to go out on the river. His overbearing caution reminded her of his son's smothered existence. There was no need to comply with what he demanded when she could see no reasonable explanation for it. She walked down to the river in the early morning half-light and jolted as she saw him quietly sitting by the boatshed. He stood up as she approached.

"Don't you have more important things to attend to, rather than sitting by the boatshed so early in the morning Mr McCray?" she asked rather curtly. It was annoying he had anticipated her excursion.

"It seems not. Thinking in the quiet is something I often neglect due to the many demands on my time. The discipline is not wasted, and today I get the bonus of a boat ride."

She grunted. "I thought you said you were not wanting to revive your nautical experiences?"

"I also said I would attend you. I am a man of my word, Miss Wick."

She had to prove her struggle to find her rhythm on her last outing was due to other factors rather than a basic lack of skill. "Well, I really can't imagine you have the experience you claim..." Today she was determined he would see the rower who had graced Fairfield halls.

As they returned to the boat-shed landing, she couldn't part ways quick enough. She needed time to think. Alone. He had matched her stroke for stroke. They had found a rhythm. The last time she had felt this familiar surge of energy was standing in Aunt Winifred's parlour after finishing a competitive event as champion. What happened on the river this morning had a recognizable feel about it, yet every fibre in her body was fighting it. She had to wonder if it was not only the rowing that had generated this aliveness in her. She wanted to ignore that idea; she wanted it to mean nothing, but it stayed, taunting her. She walked back to her lodgings, growling and kicking at the stones on the path. She must do all she could to avoid future encounters. Yet no matter how random she attempted to make her excursions to the boatshed, he was there... waiting. How could he be so persistently unyielding about this?

Encountering him at the river was unavoidable. That was very obvious. Instead, Maggie imagined the freedom of a horse-ride again: the wind through her hair; the smell of leather and linseed and horse; the sound of the saddle squeaking beneath her. She hadn't been for a ride since she had started teaching school. It seemed too long. One Sunday morning she went to the stables, but the gelding that had been made available for her was not there. Even the tack-boy was not around. As she turned to go she passed the stall holding the Captain's horse. Maggie paused and looked at him. He snorted confidently and beckoned her with a shake of his mane. It was like he knew his power of attraction. He was beautiful – and she admired his strong, masculine appeal, rubbing his forelock. "Oh, you are a handsome one," she murmured into his ear, and she opened the bolt and went inside his stall. Her hand ran down his chestnut neck and he stamped his hoof in response. "The way you stand... the way you move... I have watched you. You may think someone like me might not notice, but I do. I notice style... strength... drive..." Her hand smoothed down his mane and along his back, appreciating the raw beauty of the animal.

In a wistful moment of desire, she wondered if she had the audacity to jump on his back and ride, the feeling was overwhelming. But then, she shook herself and stepped back. There were liberties she would never take. The Captain's horse was one. "It is a shame," she said, "we would make a great duo, you and I," and she kissed him goodbye. She stepped out of the stall and pushed the bolt closed.

"Do you visit here often?" came the question, the tone clear and curious.

Maggie jumped and spun around. "Sir! I didn't realize you were there. I...um..." She blushed as she realized he most likely heard every murmured word. She abandoned herself to charm and shrugged. "I am caught."

McCray looked her up and down and noted her riding habit. "Please tell me you did not intend to take Maestro out."

"Your stallion, out for a ride? Oh, that would be incredible!"

"Yes, it would. But that was not permission. Riding Maestro is never going to happen."

"Look at him. He wants to ride. He stands there: strong, determined, so..." She stopped and blushed. Was there a blurring between Maestro and master? She turned towards the stall to hide her face. "I guess my plans for a ride today are hereby suspended. My usual horse is not here." She nodded as she left him and walked to the stable door. She could feel his eyes on her back. Was 'Inappropriate' her middle name? Her face flushed hot.

"Miss Wick?" She stopped. But didn't turn around. "I'm going out to the paddocks to check some things. If you care for a ride, you could take one of the other horses."

"Really there is no..." She flinched as she realized she sounded insolent. Why did she constantly seem to end up giving him the impression she was vulgar and ill-mannered? That was not who she was.

"You are dressed ready, and it seems you were anticipating an outing."

"I…" Now she felt stuck. She did want a ride. But with him? It wasn't at all what she was hoping for… just like the river. But then, what if he did relent and let her ride the stallion? She turned slowly and smiled. "Yes, I think that could be a refreshing diversion. You are right. I was looking forward to it."

McCray saddled a dark dun mare with a soot coloured mane. She was a gentle, placid young breeder, in between foals. Maggie rode out of the stables sedately, and McCray joined her, following the track towards the back boundary. They didn't speak for a long while. She looked at him sideways a number of times, seated astride his horse, proud and powerful. The grim line of his mouth convinced her he would never relent. He was not going to let her ride the stallion after all.

His company was uncomfortable, more so even than when they were rowing. In the boat, there was never any expectation of eye contact, but here, riding side by side she felt obliged to engage at some level. But what could she say that would not cause further embarrassment? Finally, she abandoned her attempts to work out her thoughts and cantered ahead. The smooth movement of her mare left behind the etiquette of conversation. As the wind brushed her face, a sense of blowing away the constrictions of the mundane filled her. She closed her eyes and threw back her head, relishing the feeling of the breeze rushing past. She opened her eyes and leant down on the horse's dark neck, whispering to the mare. "We are alike, you and me. They expect us to be something… but out here, there is a little bit of wild in both of us. Come on. Let's go for a run." Maggie relaxed against her neck and the mare pulled forward. Urged on by her rider, moulding and pressing against her, her canter broke into a light gallop. Maggie smiled, enjoying the way she moved, agile and free. Maggie felt a surge of vitality and the exhilaration that pulled her forward, faster. She relaxed into the moment, compelling her on. The mare responded. They raced along the track and out into a wide, lightly stocked paddock. The cattle lifted their heads and stared. She became aware of the Captain's Chestnut behind her. Maggie veered away into a scrubby knoll, flying through the trees and over logs. She broke out into a clearing, rushing for space. Maestro galloped beside her; his firm tread tracking her every move; both horses with a foamy lather over their flanks. McCray reached out, holding the mare's bridle firm, straining the strapping, and slowing the pace.

He pulled them to a stop and jumped down, grim and silent. Maggie dismounted and rubbed the mare's damp neck, whispering her thanks. She looked across at him, her eyes wild. *"That* was amazing. See I can ride. Are you sure I can't ride your stallion?" She said it to provoke him. And she knew it would.

"*That* was nothing short of idiocy!" he snapped. "And there is no way this side of eternity you will ride Maestro." He stood tall beside the animals, anger flashing in his look. "What sort of hell-bent lunacy over-took you out there? You jeopardise a good breeder, my stallion, yourself! What were you thinking?"

There was danger in his stance. It became a challenge to her, like another crazy gallop. "I was immersed in the moment." She flicked back her hair.

"Immersed? How can you be so flippant? Insanity!"

She laughed at him. "Sometimes a moment needs to be seized…"

His brow progressively became darker. He refused to be charmed. "This is virgin land you know, there are wombat and bandicoot holes everywhere. You can't treat it like an equestrian arena and expect *it* to treat you kindly Miss Wick. It demands respect."

"Respect? I have no problem with respect."

"It is blatantly obvious you do!" She turned away from him, and he grabbed her arm spinning her around to face him, his face livid. "You fly out there like this is some fashionably tended racecourse. You show no regard for the animals or yourself. Who would have to walk into class on Monday and tell the children their teacher won't be coming in? If it means you feel I am unkind, so be it."

His contentious manner took the edge off her fun. "You are being theatrical Mr McCray, like some classical Greek melodrama. No tragedy happened here today: the horses are safe."

"Certainly, through no regard from yourself, Miss Wick! This is not some storybook, where you can go back to the start and rewrite the ending if you don't like the outcome. This is real life – real people, who don't get another chance if it goes wrong. Don't *ever* do that again!"

His grip on her arm tightened and she felt her flesh pinch under his hand. She reached up and pried open his grip. "Or what? I don't get to ride your stallion? I never had a chance at that anyway!" she said, mounting the mare. Maggie turned in the saddle towards the homestead and didn't look back.

12.

"Keziah, please hand out these slates. That's lovely manners Pauline, thank you. Put away the readers because we are going to do some mathematics. I will read out the problems according to your group. Keren, I want you to practice writing the numbers zero to three on your slate while the older students do this." With the occasional groan, they started.

Maggie read out the sums and checked the progress of the groups. As she returned to the front of the class Terry squawked, and she looked up to see McCray at the back of the classroom. She was familiar with his dictum of carrying on as if he was not present, but he had not been to the classroom since her wild ride. She found it hard to stay focused. She took a deep breath and walked from one group to the next, repeating their oral problems. "Group one: two plus one; Group two..." Today he seemed unwilling to observe unobtrusively, and he paced while the tedious process of reading out sums progressed. As she glanced up between readings, she saw his eyes flash, just as they did the day, he held the horses. She sighed and resigned herself to addressing this immediately. "Wilma – I want you to come and continue. Just take it slowly: it is easier if you stand in front of each group as you read out their problem. I am up to here for the little ones. Yes, that's fine. I will be back in a moment."

Maggie walked to the back of the class and McCray gave a directive flick of his chin and headed for the verandah. "I must apologise for disrupting your lesson, but I'm sure you will understand. This matter is of the gravest concern for you."

"Me?" Maggie looked at his face bewildered. Whatever could be this pressing? "Lonnie? Sammy? Sir, you are seriously disturbing me!"

"No, no. Lonnie and Sammy are fine. This is about the school. We have a problem. I have received a letter from the Board of General Education. There has been an objection submitted – regarding the funding. They say we do not have enough students enrolled, and that..."

"This is ludicrous. We have twelve students. The minimum enrolment was reduced from fifteen a while ago. Can they just change the rules?"

"Well, given they are the Board of General Education, I think they can do what they like. But the guidelines have not changed. They are saying Jones' youngest is not eligible due to her age – she is not yet four, and so with only eleven students, they will shut it down. The funding has been withdrawn until it is investigated further."

"Keren is *nearly* four..."

He nodded slowly. "But not yet..." He waved the letter slowly.

Maggie drew her breath sharply. She suddenly realised what he was saying. "Close the school? Because of *one* student?"

McCray shrugged and presented her with the letter he held in his hand. Maggie leaned back against the verandah post for support. She tried to focus and read what it said. "This is preposterous. They had all the paperwork before we started. Jones was very definite this was all approved. Surely, they have bigger fish to fry. We are completely off the map. Who would care more about one child being too young than eleven others getting an education?" She drew a breath, her thoughts racing. "I will do it anyway. I am hardly here because provisional teaching is a lucrative occupation. Anyone knows I could earn more as a seamstress. Could Henderson's Gap possibly extend charity in meals and lodging, as abhorrent as that is for you?"

"Ouch..." he said quietly.

She stopped. "I'm sorry – that was uncalled for. I just don't know what to do. I *do* know I'm not going back in there to tell the children to go home because of some technicality. I absolutely won't."

McCray looked out at the trees and then focused on her face. "I needed to know you were still committed to this. I will get to the bottom of it. I will." He looked directly into her eyes. "In the meantime, I have to ask..."

"No! I will not! These children have done nothing to deserve this. I *am* going straight back in there to finish reading math's problems." She lightly pressed her fingers against her temples and closed her eyes. "This is absurd... random, ridiculous. God help us..." Her voice trailed off, a whisper of a prayer.

"Miss Wick, I have a request," he repeated. "It is something I have been thinking about for some time." She opened her eyes and looked at him, remembering the last time he made a request. She saw him swallow awkwardly. She followed the line of his gaze and blinked. Walking towards the schoolhouse was the grim figure of Thelma, wearing her perpetual dark grey pinafore, holding onto Alexander dressed in his Sunday best.

"Alexander is five. He is of school age. As you know, I prefer a private governess for him, so I will pay £45 per annum plus meals and lodging for that privilege. I understand your commitments here, so I am happy for him to sit in the class for his lessons. If you accept this offer, we can review the arrangement again when the enrolment numbers are confirmed with the Board and our funding is reconnected. I believe this would mean you again have a full complement of students. I'm sure we'll see new families come into the district. I hardly think this will be an ongoing issue."

That afternoon, Maggie took her hat from the stand near the door and reached for Alexander's hand to walk him back to the homestead. "How did you like your first day at school?" she asked with a smile. He said nothing. His eyes seemed to have lost the glow she had seen during the afternoon. She stopped and crouched down and turned his head towards her. "Alexander, did something not go well? You tried so hard at everything we did. I was really proud of you." Maggie paused and took a deep breath. She waited.

He stood there. Unheeded, a tear rolled down his cheek. Maggie's heart jumped up into her throat and she gently lifted her sleeve and absorbed the droplet into her cuff. She stopped herself from saying anything. Something went wrong, terribly wrong, but as she scanned the afternoon in her memory all she could see was how delighted he was. Maggie chided herself. Had she been so involved in some sort of victory dance, that she had not been able to see the needs of this little boy? She had claimed victory over the Board of General Education, and victory over McCray and the governess debacle. And in the process, a little boy cried at the end of his first afternoon in school. That was failure on a grand scale. "Oh God! I have to remember why I do this," she whispered as a prayer in her heart.

"Did the other children…?" He shook his head.

"Were the activities too hard?" He shook his head.

Maggie paused again. She could play this game for a long time and never get to the bottom of it. "Alexander, you are our first new student. Hearing what it was like at our school would help me very much."

"I..." He kicked his shoe in the dust of the walking track. Maggie waited. "I can see the school from my room," he said finally.

"Oh. You watched the children playing?"

He nodded. "I want to come back, but Dad might change his mind. I want to come tomorrow."

Maggie smiled gently, holding the weight of a little boy's heart in her hand. "Maybe he won't change his mind this time. Maybe I can ask him if you can come again. Would you like that?" He nodded seriously. "Well then. We had better get you back or Thelma will be fixing to give me a chiding for keeping you in after class. Shall we go?" She stood to her feet and held his hand as they walked around the trees towards the homestead gate. She hadn't realised the part of the main house she could see from her porch was the balcony outside Alexander's nursery. She wondered if he had watched them often. She jolted as Thelma interrupted her thoughts and bobbed a curtsy.

"Afternoon Ma'am," she said tersely. "I can see Master Alex to the homestead from here." Thelma quickly bobbed again.

"Much obliged Thelma. We'll see you tomorrow Alex." She watched them leave together, Alexander's eyes fleeting back over his shoulder as Thelma's firm hand guided him through the gate.

∿•∿

Maggie looked at the sun and decided to go for a walk. It was still early afternoon. She was quietly grateful that McCray habitually worked until dark. She sighed. Of course, she would keep her promise to Alex and speak with his father, but she was reluctant to place herself in his orbit. She felt like a planet tracking a path that was being dragged off course when he was around. It wasn't his fault. He had no idea. She just needed to gain her centre of gravity.

As she turned towards the riverbank, it seemed the memory of her excursion with Alexander to this very same spot was potent in her nostrils, like the pungent odour of smelling salts. She sat down and quietly flicked leaves onto the water that ran still and deep. An oily glaze from the sweeping leaves of bowed trees swirled in marbled rainbow patterns on the surface. She listened to lazy birdcalls in the warmth of the afternoon, and slowly replayed the day in her mind. She considered how McCray disclosed the contents of the letter. His concern genuine. She flicked another leaf onto the water and asked the questions she had not had the space to ask before. Why should he care so much? Why did it matter to him whether she was committed to this or not? Did he actually think she might not be? The questions rolled on and the answers seemed as elusive as trying to collect reflections of light on the water.

She heard him ride up and she closed her eyes, wondering momentarily if her questions had summoned him to respond. He didn't say anything until she tilted her head, shading her eyes, and smiled an acknowledgement. "Good afternoon Sir."

It was enough of an invitation to linger a moment. He dismounted Maestro lightly with military precision. "I have been riding the flats looking for strays, and here you are."

She laughed. The comment was a little clumsy, but today she was inclined to be humoured. He tethered his horse a short distance away, the sun glinting off his chestnut coat like burnished gold under water. McCray sat down on his haunches, not too close, and picked at a blade of grass. Why should these details matter? Why would she even notice them?

"Are you missing many strays?" It seemed polite to ask.

"About fifteen head. Doesn't make any sense where they could have gone. They were... never mind. We'll find them." He paused a moment and then asked, "How did Alexander go today? I was concerned he may have been a little overwhelmed."

"Your son has a reflective nature, reserved almost, yet he made a very determined effort to be part of the lessons. I was so proud of him. It is good for the younger ones to have another to share their activities. Although may I suggest Thelma chooses attire that is a little less formal? He needs to be able to run and be comfortable." McCray noted the School Ma'am report and the distance she placed between them with the official tone of her summary. She hesitated before continuing. "He was concerned he may not have the opportunity to come to class again tomorrow. I said I would talk to you."

He lowered into a seated position and stretched out his long riding boots in front of him. "Well then, if my son and his teacher both think it is a good idea, I can hardly dismiss it – given I have engaged your services to this end. I think, Miss Wick, we may actually be on the same page in this instance. Does this surprise you?"

"To be frank Sir, the whole turn of events today has me quite baffled. I admit the letter from the Board of General Education is quite disturbing – why would they go to so much trouble to shut us down? But what I find equally bizarre is your defence of our position. You have gone out of your way to protect our little school, with all its flaws. Even so far as to enrol your son. Surely you can appreciate a level of incongruency in this?" He raised his eyebrows and continued to chew his blade of grass. "Don't get me wrong, Sir, I appreciate the generosity on every level. You are offering more than my provisional teacher's wage. I just don't understand what has changed. I am still the same person. I am still Maggie Wick – the governess who only survived ten minutes in your employ previously."

McCray picked at another blade of grass and studied it intently. "Hmmm. What you say is true. Although I concede I have observed enough of you as a teacher to allay any misgivings regarding the care of my son in class. On that assessment, I feel there is more benefit for Alex being *in* your school, than just watching it morosely from his verandah lookout." He pulled out the stem of another tall blade of grass and thoughtfully chewed the tender centre. "Yes, there definitely is 'a level of incongruency', as you so articulately put it, from where I sit as well. Why would a lady – so successful in her own social circle, move back to a regional setting where opportunities are far less abundant? Why would she struggle so hard to be a provisional schoolteacher in the country when she could easily succeed in any number of endeavours elsewhere? Why would she delay the foregone conclusion of being mistress of a mansion, and tolerate the cramped quarters of a school residence? Why is she reckless off duty and yet protective while on? Why would she resign from one opportunity, and then persist at being in my employ, to the point of using duplicity and deceit to achieve that end? You see Miss Wick – you are a puzzle to me."

Maggie considered him with the faintest smile on her lips. "I fear Mr McCray you have made some rather serious miscalculations in all of your supposing."

"My exact position Miss Wick is that I have no conclusions, just questions."

"But you say it is a 'foregone conclusion' that my destiny is to be mistress of a mansion. This is a rather ill-informed assumption on your part Mr McCray."

McCray looked at her intently, saying nothing, searching for the answer to an unvoiced question.

"Fairfield Estate is hardly an option for a poverty-stricken provisional schoolteacher. It does not have the right sense of class," she said matter-of-factly.

His eyes quietly smiled at her witticism. "Miss Wick, I have not considered you to be a teacher without class. Surely the door to that parlour would be left open to you?"

She shrugged unconcerned. "Hardly. I think I have quite terminally destroyed any possibility of such an invitation. I fear I have insulted the heir of the Hastings Empire irrevocably. It appears he took my declaration of independence as an affront beyond repair."

McCray barely managed to suppress his smile. "Surely a lover's tiff and a humble apology would simply smooth the waters," he said gravely.

She looked at him and raised her brow. "Actually, I prefer waters with current and movement and depth. And that does not just refer to my love of rowing." She continued before he could say anything. "Your reckoning that I might consider offering any apology, humble or otherwise, when I was charged guilty without cause is not likely. I can assure you that my rejection of the murky Hastings waters is not the fickle result of an inconsequential 'tiff', nor is it the simple matter you suppose. Smoothing them is not something I am interested in pursuing."

"It seems I have seriously underestimated the complexity of the issues." This time he did allow himself to smile. "The incongruencies remain. The puzzle continues. The questions go unanswered; back to square one." He had one answer though… and that alone was particularly satisfying.

"You flatter me rather undeservingly, Mr McCray. I don't suppose I am quite as complicated as you would have me believe. However, if it amuses you to think thus, I will do my best to live up to the mystery."

"Oh, I have no doubt you are a mystery, Miss Wick. But then I do flatter myself to possess commendable skills at unravelling intriguing riddles. And like all good riddles, they are not quite so random as perhaps they might first seem. There is usually a solution."

She laughed. "I feel like I have just been challenged to a Chinese puzzle tournament... or a spelling bee... or a good game of chess. But you may be surprised, Mr McCray. Lonnie taught me Tangrams on her knee; I was spelling bee runner-up in my school and I have won my own share of chess games in drawing rooms around town." She held his gaze intently, trying to read what he might be thinking. It disturbed her, not just a little bit, that he did not give the slightest hint as to what was going on. "Or is poker your game of choice?" she asked rather reproachfully.

He laughed lightly. "Ahh, I am indeed a poker player of mark. Still, the idea of chess intrigues me. I tell you what: I challenge you to a game, in the library, after dinner Wednesday night. You have to eat anyway. We might as well share a meal before a bloodied battle of wits."

"You forget Sir, Wednesday night is Sammy and Lonnie's night off. And I don't cook on school nights."

His smile broadened. "I did not forget. I would never take advantage of your family's good cooking to lure you to a tournament. That would hardly be mannerly. I can make a light fare that will suffice for sustenance. It will hardly compare to Lonnie's meals, but you already know she is unsurpassed as a cook." Was he really inviting her to a meal he would prepare himself? She felt her orbit wobble. It was an invitation she struggled to refuse. When he asked, "Will I tell Alexander to expect company for our Wednesday night special?" she felt her steadfastness dissolve completely.

"Sir, I feel at a complete disadvantage, except on one account: I *can* play chess. You may indeed have to resort to spoiling the food or spilling the drinks to keep the playing field level."

He seemed satisfied. He stood to his feet and bowed formally. "Wednesday evening it is; five o'clock. I look forward to it." He mounted Maestro and rode off. Maggie noted with a smile that he left the way he had come, the strays forgotten. Perhaps he was not such a good poker player after all.

13.

As Wednesday night approached, Maggie was in a fever of anxiety. Was it beyond the realms of decency for her to accept such an invitation? She felt she had been pulled completely off course by some mesmeric influence. Was she playing with fire? She didn't doubt it for a moment. But this wasn't the intense rage she feared the last time she dined at this man's house. This was much more insidious, perhaps no less destructive.

Lonnie poured a cup of tea for herself. In her preoccupation, she forgot to pour one for Maggie. She sat in the kitchen sighing. "Chess? This is not good… This is not good…"

"Lonnie, a game of chess is not so bad. It is not like I'm playing Strip Poker. Chess is very respectable."

"Missy! Chess is a game of intellect, like the Chinese Mahjong – it takes skill to play. You see what he is; and he see you."

Sammy was less philosophical. "Perhaps he just wants to play a game of Chess."

Lonnie glared at him and huffed. "Don't be ridiculous. No man just want to play Chess."

Maggie was surprised by McCray's willingness to play. Perhaps he was not half competent himself. She shrugged. It was kind of curious.

Lonnie was not finished. "A man despise skill, especially in a lady! They don't want clever. You never see him again." Her train of logic seemed to satisfy her. "Good idea. Yes. Go play your game, Missy. Show your skill. Show him you clever."

Maggie grimaced. Duncan McCray may consider himself skilled at solving riddles, but what if she did lose the game? If that happened, the man she found herself puzzling over, may be no less revealed. Her motivation to win went up a notch. She had to see if there was anything behind his poker-player mask.

Lonnie had pressed a modest, plain white frock for her; she wore a shawl around her shoulders. Maggie thought it would send a message about the serious nature of the tournament. She was not going to be frivolous about this venture, even if it came under the guise of a friendly game of intellects.

He was in the kitchen when she arrived. It was the tradition of the house that Wednesdays were 'staff-day-off'. When management had access to the kitchen this one evening of the week, it generally created more distress for Lonnie than any benefit afforded from having the break. Sammy discretely arranged to visit friends this night and they were both away. Maggie was quietly grateful to Sammy for that. Alexander sat on the kitchen table watching his father do battle with a whisk and duck eggs. McCray glanced up as Maggie came through the door. "Duck egg omelettes tonight; a light meal. I don't want to stifle the competitive energy needed for our game."

Maggie checked the wood stove – which was burning adequately and went to the pantry and brought out a selection of chives, onions, tomatoes and capsicums.

McCray looked at the assortment with approval. "Cheese is a favourite of mine. I negotiated with Lonnie to have some tonight. She said it was on the top shelf to the right." Lonnie governed her cheeses with the precision required of this valuable homemade commodity. Maggie turned in the pantry and rolled her eyes. Of course, she knew where Lonnie stored her precious cheeses. "Do you care to eat here or in the dining room, Miss Wick? The choice is yours since you are our guest."

Maggie considered for a moment. Would McCray be more comfortable in the dining room, or here in the serving quarters? It was easy to assume the dining room would be less taxing on his sense of the familiar. "Here would be lovely, thank you."

"I agree, Miss Wick, less formal."

She smiled tersely. Had he seen through her little logical progression? If so, he gave no indication. It seemed he was making every effort to be affable and pleasant. Her determination to win almost seemed ruthless in the light of his good humour.

"This won't take long; into the pan." Alex tossed his chosen ingredients into the mixture, while Maggie cut some bread and made fried toast. In no time it was flipped, and Alex sat at the table eating while the next omelette was poured. Maggie pulled up a chair and sat with Alex, who was chatting about Terry the Cockatoo while he ate. The school pet was a favourite with him. McCray watched as Maggie listened to Alex mimicking his classmates' very rudimentary attempts to teach Terry parrot-talk. He splattered his omelette and she laughed and reached out to wipe his mouth with a serviette. McCray froze momentarily by the stove and then started banging the pan with the egg flip firmly. Maggie could sense the energy coming from his quarter. It was disconcerting having him standing there in his casual black house clothes as if this was normal. It was anything but normal. She wished she had dressed up and demanded they eat in the dining room. If only she could rewind and start again. In fact,…

McCray put two plates on the table with cutlery. "It is nice of you to join us, Miss Wick. Even a soldier can pull together a meal given the motivation."

"Thank you for the invitation. Even a schoolteacher can dine in comfort, whatever the setting," countered Maggie primly. What was this insistence on soldiering? That was not who he was now, and she wasn't going to let him forget who she was either. He might be able to scrub together a meal in a mess-tent or a homestead, just as she was comfortable in the familiar setting of a farm kitchen, or a formal banquet hall.

He looked at her and tilted his head slightly. "Shall we say grace and eat?" he offered. She bowed her head and he gave thanks. He took up his serviette and said, "Please. Before it gets cold."

Maggie had no idea an omelette could take so long to eat. If being in the scullery was intended to create a sense of unease in her opponent, it certainly didn't appear to be taking effect. His gaze seemed to burn holes through her head, yet she could not quite determine what it was that unnerved her so. She refused to let his intensity put her off her game and was determined to keep the conversation light and safe. Alex was the only safe person in the room at this moment, so she made sure she kept everything bright and included him in every comment, every reflection, every laugh, every observation. She was not one to hold to the maxim that children should be seen and not heard. Finally, McCray rose and required Alex to say his goodnights. It was time for bed.

Maggie went to the Library while McCray took his son upstairs. She pushed open the heavy door and remembered the first time she had laid eyes on this man. She smiled slightly at the dullness of the wax sheen on the polished floorboards, scolded by the broken teapot. In the centre of the room was a small, round occasional table inlaid with a parquetry chessboard, the timber grains skilfully angled to create a three-dimensional illusion. Even to Maggie's untrained eye, she could see this table was a craftsman's masterpiece, as were the carved ivory and ebony pieces set out in the precision of a military parade. McCray's office chair was pushed up to the table facing the door and a drawing room chair sat opposite, ready to do battle. The chesterfield lounge had been spun around so it faced the chess table with a cushion propped against one arm.

This was not a haphazard arrangement of pushing aside some ledgers on his manager's desk to make room for a game board as she might have expected, this had taken time and consideration. The game table stood out like a wrestling ring. All that was needed was a hazy rabble of gambling spectators and the effect would have been complete. She circled it carefully, taking it all in. Maggie reached out and picked up a black rook. She twirled it softly in her hands, caressing the craftsmanship with admiration. This was stunning. She glanced up to see McCray by the door watching her intently. She smiled. "I was just admiring your Castle, Sir."

"Mine?" he said, pausing momentarily, as he came towards her. "So, you know I only play black?"

Without hesitation and a beguiling shrug, she said, "Oh, I had no idea... I just know I always play White." *A blind man could see you intended to play black by the way the chairs are positioned,* she thought. "Shall we?" He only nodded as he poured them both some limewater from a decanter on a tray near the chesterfield.

"White moves first," he said as he held the chair for her. A delicious shiver ran across her shoulders as she sat. She loved healthy competition, and she pulled in her shawl just a little.

"Let the game begin." Maggie glanced at the fob watch pendant around her neck. She felt a thrill when she took a bishop; a note of dismay when both his knights fell; full out irritation when his rook surrendered. It took exactly twenty-two minutes and forty-five seconds for her to call checkmate.

She got up and took a swallow of limewater, shaking her head. She turned around. "What was that?"

He leaned back in his chair, a little smug smile playing around his eyes. "I think that was a trouncing in anybody's terms."

"It was not! You insult me! You cannot even play badly and hide it. One sound move, and two false? Surely you could have shown a little more ingenuity?"

"Was it not your ambition to win? You have won."

Her shawl fell to the floor as she swallowed more water, her face flushed. "I didn't win anything, and you know it. You could have just said you didn't want to be bothered."

"Oh, but I did want to be bothered. I have anticipated our game most assuredly."

"Then why the farce Sir? You mock me?"

"Miss Wick, I don't think I would be so brave."

"Seems to me Sir, you have very clearly shown that audacity."

"Some soldiers, and although you think this history of mine has no relevance to my current station... some soldiers engage a strategy of allowing their opponent to show their hand, take some losses, lose a battle so the war can be won."

"Tosh and twaddle. You have no idea what I am capable of because there was absolutely no field on which to demonstrate it."

"So, you agree?"

"Agree? I agree to nothing!"

He went over and picked up his glass, swirling a wedge of lime in the water. He said nothing. She stared at him openly irritated. He returned her gaze, his eyes appreciating the candour he saw there. He held her scrutiny while he sipped the water in his glass. She didn't disappoint him.

"Agree to what?"

"I merely offer a rematch. One more to your taste." He repositioned her King and Queen.

"A rematch? You want to do that again? I don't think so."

"Fair play... head to head... to the death... no holds barred. Show me what you can do Miss Wick. I am intrigued." He held up his rook from where it had been taken captive and put it back in position. The board was reset.

"If I win, I will not do this again."

"Then I give you my word: I will do what I can to see that does not happen again. It sounds like you *want* to lose? I find that hard to believe of you."

"I don't believe for a second I will lose." She drained her glass of water and sat down. She noted the time on her fob watch and made her first move. Time slowed to the rhythm of the game. She became absorbed in the strategy; the combat of wills. The first piece to go was hers. Somewhere in the evening, the patter of Alex's bare feet came into the library. McCray nodded to his son and he curled up on the chesterfield lounge, with the cushion under his tousled head and a much-loved teddy with a threadbare ear tucked under his arm. Maggie quietly got up and retrieved her shawl where it lay forgotten on the floor and pressed it gently under his chin. Alex smiled sleepily and closed his eyes as she resumed her seat. McCray stared at the board immobilised. It seemed to take some time for him to exhale slowly and make a move. It cost him a knight.

When the mantle clock struck ten he stood to his feet. "Miss Wick, a grazier's life starts early in the morning. Unfortunately, I will be unable to finish this tonight: you put up a formidable fight. However, I would very much appreciate it if you would consider continuing this game next Wednesday… same time?"

Maggie looked up at him over the chessboard. He glanced at his son sleeping on the lounge. "Give me a minute, I will walk you to your quarters." He scooped Alex into his arms and carried him out. He returned with a warm throw and wrapped it around her shoulders. They said nothing as they walked back to the schoolhouse. He paused at the step. "I really did appreciate your company this evening Miss Wick."

"You're welcome," she said quietly. And he nodded thoughtfully, turned and disappeared into the dark.

Maggie lit the lamp on her nightstand and sat on her bed. She closed her eyes. The image of the chessboard was burnt into her vision. "Oh dear," she thought to herself, "this is very confronting for my Minotaur." She picked up the book of Greek Mythology that had been on the teacher's desk the morning Leon came to her classroom. Until now she had shown very little curiosity as to how it came to be there. She suspected the messenger might have been the custodian of the Henderson library, the giver of whistles, the guardian of river rowers, the rider of stallions, the player of Chess.

She turned to the frontispiece again and considered the print. She had existed for such a long time with this dangerous labyrinth, and the uneasy, unearthly, unruly monster she associated with relationships. Did she even want the Minotaur slain who devoured young maidens sent to appease its appetites? Could she live with an idea... a reality... that was less dangerous, less intriguing, more human? Who was her Theseus who would finally slay this monster?

In the engraving plate, the Minotaur stood snorting viciously from its prison at the centre of the Cretan Labyrinth. She studied the expression on Theseus' face emerging to slay the Minotaur. She jolted as it seemed there was something strangely familiar about Theseus' intense gaze. Why would a relationship with this man be any more feasible than Fairfield with all its privilege? How could the outcome be any different? On both accounts, it hardly could be seen as rational. She tallied up a mental ledger.

His position: a military man of rank. Her position... or lack of it.

His background: he told Hastings stories of society and affluence. Her background: an orphan raised by an uncle and a Chinese housekeeper; educated by a childless, widowed aunt.

There was history: he has a child. But there was a loud silence around the circumstances of his wife.

She was naïve, with no experience to speak of: an untrained provisional schoolteacher.

But most of all: it was eminently clear, they could not, would not, agree on anything. Therein lies the difference to Fairfield. No longer would she bow her head and say "yes", when her whole body screamed "no". And she knew, eventually, *they* did not take kindly to "no". If she was honest: the ledger did not add up. She snapped the book shut and threw it into the corner. It was ridiculous to even think she would be of interest to him in "that" way. The invitation was just part of his compulsive need to unravel puzzling riddles. He said so himself.

Well, she was going to win the game of Chess and then have nothing to do with the man again. Except whatever was required in his responsibilities regarding the school; or as her landlord; or as a parent of one of her students; and ah yes, he was also her parents' employer. She sighed. It seemed he was embroiled in her life at every turn. As she rolled into bed and pummelled her pillow in place, she wondered again if Henderson's Gap was indeed big enough for both of them.

When she woke the next morning, she padded out onto the verandah in the early mist to visit the outhouse. By the lattice door, was a pillowcase folded at the top. She opened it and found her shawl rolled neatly inside. She pulled it out and held the softness to

her face, and she could feel the breath of Alex on it.
There was a small card that read:

> *"Incongruencies abound...*
> *Every move astounds...*
> *Looking forward to next week's round."*

It was simply signed "D".

Now she knew, without a doubt, Minotaur and
Theseus would do battle on a chessboard, and the
outcome would determine her destiny.

14.

Maggie changed into her gown and watched the layers of tantalising ice-blue fabric fall softly to the floor. She smoothed the lace along the neckline and over her shoulders and turned to check herself in Lonnie's battered mirror. Sammy took Lonnie visiting every Wednesday night while they played chess. Lonnie fought the outings violently. This night she particularly asserted her need to be here to help curl Maggie's hair. Sammy insisted she would manage. It was not often Sammy put his foot down, but when he did, all of Lonnie's bluster came to naught.

There was a hint of mischief lingering in Maggie's eyes as she fastened her earrings and a matching pendant. When her things arrived from Aunt Winifred's, she found the ensemble she had worn to an annual charity ball. That night she had been hailed Belle of the Ball, so it was on reputable social authority that this gown worked well with her figure and dark hair. It felt brazen to wear something as stunning as this, for a Wednesday night game of chess. Would McCray be thrown by the incongruence? She didn't want to confess it, but it was a test. Would he start feigning and simpering over her beauty? Would he mock her or ignore her efforts entirely, and be heartlessly immune to her charms? If he did either, he could not be her Theseus. She didn't need another feeble hero who was unable to stand against the monster.

She came down the stairs on the stroke of five. Alex was standing near the bottom, looking awkward in a starched white collared shirt, a little vest, long trousers and boots. When he looked up and saw her his face lit up, openly admiring her, and he seemed to relax. Maggie curtsied, smiled at him and put her finger to her lips. "Shhh…"

"Alex, I want you to…" said McCray as he came through the door. He was dressed impeccably in his military dress uniform and his polished boots clicked the flagstone floor sharply as he stopped, standing stock-still. She was aware of how confidently he bore himself in the handsome regalia of rank. She felt just a little unnerved: full dress uniform and a ballroom gown? They both had the same idea? Questions crowded her mind, as she stood there unable to move. The pause seemed to suspend time.

Eventually, she stepped down the final couple of stairs, and McCray came forward formally and took her gloved hand and bent over it. "Ma'am I forget myself. Welcome." He could well have been at the reception of a gala event, not in the stairwell of his serving staff. "May I suggest one of us is miserably under-dressed on this occasion?"

That was not at all what she was expecting, and she laughed softly, acknowledging him with a regal nod and a curtsy. "Sir, I will do my utmost to ensure I take a little more care next Wednesday."

He looked into her eyes, reflecting silver-blue from her dress. "I doubt you could make any improvement on perfection. The effect is entirely enchanting." He smiled slightly. "However, what gratifies me most is that you consider there will be yet another Wednesday; that you predict our contest will be continued."

"I will guarantee," she said confidently, "I will do all in my power not to lose tonight, just like any other night."

"Ahh... but it has been weeks. What *if* tonight is the night? What if tonight I win?" he asked teasingly.

"I would demand a rematch, best of three, to recoup my dignity."

"I'd be happy to oblige, although I don't believe your dignity is in any danger Miss Wick, regardless of how the Chess pieces fall. Come, tonight we dine in the Sitting Room. Knowing your propensity for comfort, and disinclination for formality, the Dining Room seemed a little cavernous for just three. Alex, lead the way."

He offered her a drink. "If you don't mind, I thought we might dine straight away, so there is more time for the game. Alex, come and help carry the dishes." They left and Maggie surveyed the sitting room, taking it all in. The room was reorganised and a small table with a white cloth was set for three by the fireplace. "Oh, he is good..." she thought apprehensively, "suave, in every detail." She felt herself being drawn down the labyrinth, and she desperately needed a ball of red thread so she could unravel her way out. Suddenly she felt disorientated; the labyrinth was confusing and impossible to navigate.

They returned and McCray held her chair while she sat. They said grace and he removed the meal-covers. "Salt beef and potatoes; bread and jam for dessert."

Maggie's laugh tinkled like the soft bells of a wind-chime. She had to give him star-chart credits for this. He played the Incongruence Game better than anyone she knew. That he would serve the common drover's camp staple by candlelight with silver cutlery had a sublime sense of disparity. To be honest, she thought, Lonnie's special roast duck would have seemed oddly out of place. But if he thought he would get a reaction that would throw her game, she determined he certainly would be disappointed. "I am touched by the indulgence to reminisce my childhood. I haven't enjoyed a meal like this in years." She picked up her fork and ate it delicately as if it were a chef's tantalising speciality. "And, Lonnie's plum-and-melon jam is famous in this district. You could not have made a more discerning choice."

"I'm glad," he said warmly, nodding to acknowledge her parry. "Alex was thinking something else might be preferred, but I said, 'You know, let's just keep it simple.'"

Maggie looked him directly in the eye and said, "Simple it is not. Amusing perhaps, but definitely anything but simple."

He met her penetrating gaze with a slight tilt of his head, and Maggie felt the colour rise in her cheeks. "Oh, I agree with you wholeheartedly, Miss Wick. At least it's not bland."

After dinner, Alex was read a story in the library. Maggie sat on the chesterfield lounge, looking thoughtfully at the board, while McCray took his son up to bed. She wondered where this game they were playing was going. McCray paused when he came into the room, openly admiring her as she looked up from the book she was holding. "I would consider it a waste when we are dressed for a ball, not to have at least one dance."

Maggie tilted her head slightly. Since the moment she walked down the stairs, he had matched her on every move. Just like chess. But she hadn't expected this invitation to dance. She stood up. "Just like chess, Sir, I *can* dance. I'm just wondering whether I want to."

"You chose the ball gown, did you not?"

"You chose military dress. Does that mean you want a war?"

He smiled. "It feels like you want to fight, and I want to dance. Is there a solution to this dilemma?"

"You are the one who likes an intriguing puzzle."

"Hmm." He held out his hand. "How about we both get what we want: one waltz for me; then we can do war on the chessboard."

"Now why would *you* want to dance?"

"To satisfy myself I can still keep time."

"No other reason?"

He considered that and shrugged. "I have been out of social circulation for a while. My insecurities are showing. Your timing is impeccable and might be just what I need."

"Well if nothing else, the flattery is endearing, although you have no experience with my timing."

"Oh, I think I do…" he murmured softly, as she took his offered hand and he led her to the drinks cabinet where he wound a little music box that sat there. It tinkled a waltz, and in the quiet of the library, they danced around the floor. As the music slowed to a stop, they paused awkwardly, looking into each other's face. She stepped out of his arms and curtsied slowly as she tried to regain her equilibrium.

He looked at her soberly. "I was right. Your timing is perfect." He walked over to the drinks cabinet and closed the lid on the music box and poured two drinks. He came back and offered her the glass. "Now to war…" and he pulled out her chair to resume their Chess game. Again, Alex padded his way into the room at some point during the evening and curled up on the chesterfield with his bear and went back to sleep. McCray had a rug folded ready and got up and tucked it in around Alex's shoulders.

At ten o'clock he predictably rose and apologised for cutting the evening short. As he took Alex back upstairs Maggie went to Lonnie's rooms and paused and looked into Lonnie's rather battered cheval dress mirror. She had wondered whether the discipline of his weekday evening curfew would be conceded tonight; but no... not to be. She wondered what other restraints he was very strict about. She changed her gown for the walk back to her quarters.

McCray said nothing until he released her hand on the step of the schoolhouse. "Miss Wick, I need you to know I will be seeking an audience with Sammy this week. To delay discussing my intentions, I feel would be unseemly. I trust that would be acceptable with you."

Maggie lifted her head. A million doubts and questions flew to the tip of her tongue, but before she could find the strength to articulate even one, he turned on his heel and was gone.

15.

Maggie had Sammy help plot out some garden beds on Saturday. She drew lines in the dirt in front of the verandah of the schoolhouse and Sammy used his crowbar to loosen the dirt, compacted from years of traffic. They dragged in some narrow logs and pegged them to define the garden bed, which would hopefully keep little feet at bay. Sammy had systematically catalogued a seed collection and Maggie was given full reign to choose what she wanted. She already had decided on bright marigolds, and sunflowers they could harvest for Terry. Then a practical streak came into play and she added vegetables to the planned bank of colour. She thought the children would enjoy harvesting beans and beets and radishes from their garden as well. Sammy shook his head. It broke all the conventions of real gardening, but he had learnt not to argue with Maggie when she had that particular set to her jaw.

They watered down the clods of dirt and Sammy brought in barrows of his compost and mixed in manure to give the soil a boost. Sammy had rules about garden bed preparation, and Maggie deferred to his experience. After all, his vegetables were legendary.

He made up some portable seedbeds out of packing boxes, so the children could plant the seeds she selected. He instructed Maggie to get the kids to turn the bed with their trowels and to continue to break down the clods with water and their digging sticks. He reassured Maggie by the time the seedlings were ready to transplant, the soil in the garden bed would be welcoming them.

It had been an industrious, satisfying morning. They sat in the shade of the tank-stand drinking lemonade and snacking on the date cake Lonnie had sent for morning tea. Sammy focused on a crumb in his hand and casually remarked. "The Captain spoke to me yesterday."

Maggie was instantly alert. "Summoned to the office. Have you been naughty?"

"I'm too old for naughty." Sammy smiled in his laidback way. "He fancies you, Missy."

Maggie hardly knew how to respond, and the heat from the morning exertions made her face feel flushed. Then Sammy added, "He wants permission to go courting, although in my mind he is already well down that road."

"What did you say?"

Sammy paused and considered something. He shrugged. "What could I say? The man had made up his mind. He didn't say it outright, but I could have got the impression if Lonnie and me want to stay at Henderson's Gap it might be…"

He hadn't finished before Maggie jumped to her feet. "What? He resorts to blackmail? This is outrageous! Would he really stoop so low to extract your consent? As if somehow this would sanction whatever he wants! That insufferable man! He has entirely no grounds on which to terminate your arrangement. He has got to be kidding if he thinks he can roll my family over a barrel to play Chess on a Wednesday night!" She stood there astounded. The audacity of his power-play shocked her back to reality.

Sammy considered her thoughtfully. "So, Lonnie was right. It's not just Chess."

"Even if you gave consent, I certainly will not! Is he seriously so oblivious to the fact I am not just an incidental detail to this scenario? There is absolutely no way, should all hell freeze over, I could ever pursue a relationship with a man like that! Monster!" He could no longer masquerade as Theseus; he was the Minotaur himself.

Sammy offered a quiet, "Well that's a relief." He didn't seem at all disturbed by the situation.

"You are absolutely right! It is a relief. I cannot believe I was actually getting duped into considering such a thing could be possible. Idiot! Fool! I am completely embarrassed." She turned and stormed off. Sammy nibbled on another piece of date cake and poured himself a mug of lemonade and watched unperturbed as she fumed and paced under the trees.

Eventually, she came back and sat under the tank stand. "Sammy I am so sorry. I had no idea you and Lonnie might be jeopardised by this. I will do what I can to make sure you are okay."

"I'm sure we'll be fine. Are you done?"

Maggie looked at him shocked, anger firing her irises large and black. "No! I am not done. There is no way this is finished."

"Well, I've got something to say."

Maggie blinked. Already Sammy had said more than he would normally say in a week.

"You are my girl. Always and always. That a man would set his sights on you, is ambitious, to say the least. In my opinion, that Fair-paddock fellow was a right..."

"Fairfield..."

"Yeah... whatever he calls himself, he didn't have the gumption to acknowledge your family; much less offer us the common courtesy to share the fine detail he was planning a proposal of marriage. The Captain gets points just for asking." Maggie went to interject, but Sammy held up his hand. "The Captain is not taking this lightly. I'm not blind Maggie. He's been fighting with himself ever since you arrived. But you are so quick to think the worst of him. I purposely never said he did anything untoward, yet you've drawn and quartered him without so much as a pause."

"But you said...!"

"I said: 'The man had made up his mind. He *didn't say* anything outright, but I *could* have got the *impression* if Lonnie and me want to stay at Henderson's Gap it *might* be…'"

"You practised that. You set me up!"

"If you had defended him against the charges, or shrugged it off, I would have figured there was nothing more to be said…" He brushed the crumbs off his hands and helped himself to another slab of date loaf. "As it is, you don't have a clue. You need to know him, Maggie, be sure of his character before you decide whether he is going to be the one for you. The God Almighty doesn't match us with imbeciles or mongrels. Generally, we make those choices ourselves. That is why I gave my consent. Not because I think it's a done deal, but Missy, you need to know who you're dealing with. *Then* you can make your choice." He grinned. "I *do* know it's not just chess though; chess never got a reaction like that, even out of you."

She shook her head as if clearing away some evil mist. "You mean he actually asked? He didn't force your hand?"

"If he was my own flesh and blood, I couldn't have been more proud of his manner."

"But you said he had already made up his mind."

"Well, I don't think he would have said anything at all… unless he had determined in himself what he wanted. Do you? It is not his way."

"But what if you had said 'No'?"

Sammy drained his cup and shrugged. "Huh, I wonder. Perhaps there is a lot more still to discover." He smiled as he tucked his mug back in his canvas lunch bag.

"Sammy! I believe you are on his side! Has the man put a spell on you?"

"Missy, I'm on nobody's side except'n yours. I don't want you sabotaging something that could be good before you have a chance to see what it is. And I don't want you marrying a cur either. You did well in missing Long-paddock. It might be the same with the Captain, but you have the right to give yourself the best chance to make sure you know which it is. Then, at least, whatever life throws at you, you have character and trust."

Sammy stood to his feet. "I believe the seedbeds are done. Ready for planting." He picked up his crowbar and shovel that were leaning against the tank-stand and added them to the things in his wheelbarrow. "Time to get your garden-bed ready; watching things grow is a rewarding pursuit," he said drily as he made his way back to the homestead.

16.

About every three months, an itinerant minister came to Henderson's Gap and conducted Church. It seemed a bit like a Queen's holiday picnic because the whole station downed tools and attended. There was no guarantee exactly when he would be back, and it usually was not on a Sunday. Each family would bring a meal to share with the clergy after the service.

This was the first time they were able to hold Church in the schoolhouse. It was a change that caused much excitement because it was so much more fitting than the horse stables. They would have real seats, instead of sitting on bundled hay stooks. The school-desks were moved out of the way, and a little portable organ brought down from the drawing room. A pulpit was fashioned from a couple of stacked crates covered with a white cloth. A vase of geraniums sat on Maggie's desk, disguised under a white tablecloth, and pushed back into the corner. The elements of Holy Communion were covered with starched lace. Maggie was amazed at how quickly her classroom was transformed into a sacred sanctuary.

Well before the service time, McCray came and knocked on the lattice door of Maggie's quarters.

"Sorry to disturb you Miss Wick, but I do come bearing a gift." Maggie looked sceptically at the rather nondescript box he held in his hand. She tried not to think suspiciously of the offering or the giver. Sammy's words rang in her head, and she admonished herself, "Do not think the worst; give him a chance." But it was already Monday and he had not spoken to her or made any effort to engage her in conversation since their chess game last week. She wondered if he had decided after his conversation with Sammy it was against his better judgement to pursue "courtship". Given their turbulent start, she could hardly be surprised.

She wordlessly took the wooden box and opened the lid. Embedded in a purple cloth nest, was a teacher's handbell. Her guard dropped, and he noticed with satisfaction that her eyes light up. "A school bell!" Then she remembered. "Oh. I don't think I thanked you for the whistle."

"Hmm," he agreed nonchalantly. "No offence taken. It is only solid silver; only a family heirloom; only given to me by my Grandfather." He chuckled at the surprise in her eyes. "It is…. well, it really was a gift from my grandfather. I guess it only becomes an heirloom when I pass it on to my son."

"Belated, but thank you. I thought it was a brilliantly simple solution to my dilemma. You can give it to Alex now." She wound the red cord of the whistle into his hand before she lifted out the bell and it chimed clear. "Thank you for this. Really. I didn't expect such a plain box to hold something so wonderful." He could not doubt her sincerity.

"Duly noted: gifts need to come in a box that is preferably not plain."

"A silver whistle; books of Greek Mythology; this beautiful bell. And I... I haven't given you a thing. That is rather recalcitrant of me."

This time he laughed. It was a pleasure to hear him truly just laugh; relaxed and amused. "Oh, I wouldn't say that. The mop bucket, for instance, that's an example of what has been given to me since you arrived."

"Oh that," she shrugged. "Now that was an irresistible gesture of cordial appreciation. Who could resist a gift like that?"

He looked at her, his gaze softening. "I tried. I really did." He straightened up and adjusted his collar. "Could I visit with you later, after the Church luncheon? I would like to talk some, but I need to go now – the minister is waiting. I thought it might be fitting to use the bell this morning, as a call to worship?"

"I think that would be perfect." He turned to go, and she called out as he strode down the steps. "Duncan?" He stopped mid-stride, jarring as if something had shot through his chest. He turned to face her. "Thank you," she said.

He nodded. "You're welcome, Maggie. I will see you after lunch."

❧•❧

Maggie played the hymns on the little organ. The Reverend served Holy Communion, dedicated a baby, offered up prayers, read from the Holy Scriptures, preached his sermon, and baptised Priscilla and one of the jackaroos in the river. Sometimes he did a wedding; rarely a funeral because death is not always so convenient so as to coincide with his stopovers. But he did visit a grave and offer some belated words of comfort to the bereaved. Maggie thought it had the feel of a spiritual spring-clean: with every possible spiritual sacrament being taken out, dusted off and partaken of, to be put back on the shelf until next time he came through.

She was sitting on one of the benches under the trees in the schoolyard nibbling on a last remaining biscuit. The trestle tables looked like they had been hit by a swarm of locusts with only crumbs on the cloth, and a few isolated plates to suggest the bountiful buffet of sandwiches, savoury pies, dampers and other easy to handle foods that had been served. It seemed a pity to only celebrate the goodness of God together when the overworked and under-resourced ordained man of God passed through on his circuit.

Even to Maggie, his sermonic insights seemed a little trite, when compared to Jones' perpetually searching explorations. Jones didn't have the formal schooling of the minister, but should that exclude him from encouraging others in their Faith? And then it occurred to her, regardless of any official endorsement, this is what Jones did every day with his family and his friends. He had the heart, if not the robes, of a shepherd.

Olivia stepped around the trees, avoiding the gathering of worker's families at the tables. Maggie moved over and offered her a seat. "I enjoyed church today. It was very different to the cathedral I attended with Aunt Winifred." She grinned. "And I know Tom appreciated not having to do a Maths lesson. It was lovely Priscilla was baptised." Olivia looked out at the sliver leafed trees that stood behind the schoolhouse and shifted awkwardly on the edge of the bench. Maggie looked at her dark eyes and saw sadness there. "I'm sorry. You don't seem so delighted about today's proceedings."

Olivia's attention snapped back. Her voice was soft. "Priscilla wanted to be baptised – it was good she had the opportunity to do that, like Jesus in the Jordan."

Maggie paused. "Oh." She had no idea how to proceed with the conversation. She looked over at the tables and noticed how everyone was still energetically engrossed in discussions. It was rather a unique situation for Maggie; the one who smoothly engaged total strangers in the ballroom was struggling to sustain a conversation under some trees. The shade had moved, and now the table stood in full sun. It really was too warm to join those standing at the buffet table. She swallowed and thought she might like a drink of water. She sat with that thought for a moment and fanned her face but didn't really feel motivated to do anything about it. She could not see Jones or McCray or the minister anywhere. She guessed they had adjourned to the big house for more comfortable discussions. She wondered how long she needed to wait before she too could politely excuse herself and leave. No one had made any attempt to remove dishes or clear the tables.

Olivia looked towards the trestle-table for a moment and then kicked at the dust near her feet. "Do you know what they speak of?" she asked.

Maggie glanced at Liv, who quickly averted her eyes. "Whatever it is, it seems to have created a level of interest in the ranks."

Olivia paused and then quietly said, "They are talking about us. It doesn't matter to them that our family lives here. They think our children should be included."

"Your kids are great. Each one of them has so many strengths. Priscilla particularly is mature and smart for one so young." Maggie thought how beautiful Olivia was in that moment, and for the first time, she didn't feel betrayed by Jones' devotion to her. "I was thinking just now – we should have Church more often than once every blue moon when the minister comes around. Jones could teach us. Obviously, some basic theology wouldn't go astray here. He could do that."

Olivia smiled affectionately. She was proud of her husband and charmed by Maggie's naivety. She had missed the point completely. Olivia shifted her weight, and Maggie noticed the swelling of another pregnancy starting to show. "Maggie, I really believe you have no idea. They are talking about the takings."

❧•❧

Maggie had no opportunity to clarify what Olivia meant, because Jones came, and they left together. When McCray invited Maggie for a walk soon afterwards, she felt the same sense of reprieve she saw in Olivia's eyes. He took her arm and escorted her away from the schoolhouse.

There was no apparent direction or purpose in the path he chose. Maggie glanced at his face as they strode along the dusty track. He seemed distracted, as if this was the last thing he particularly wanted to do at this moment. She felt an annoyance rise in her chest, a bit like winning that first game of Chess. Honestly, he should have just postponed the invitation or not bothered at all if her presence was such a burden. She was certainly not pining to be in the company of one who considered her a social inconvenience. She took a deep breath and reminded herself again of Sammy's wisdom. She tried to think of a clever way to break the stony silence. All she could think to say was an inane "So, the bell seemed to work: The Church service went well."

He grunted.

She tried again, perhaps something a little more personal. "The baptisms in the river; I thought they were very meaningful. Perhaps because they reminded me of my own baptism, just before I left to go to school."

He sighed, and said a generic, "Hmm, I'm glad you thought so."

"Also, I found the public hanging just before lunch a nice touch to the day's program."

He assented again. "Sure. Very pleasant."

Maggie stopped and withdrew her arm. "Really? Because to be honest Mr McCray, if you cannot make an effort to at least be polite I will happily leave you to your thoughts. You don't have to do this, and neither do I. Please Sir, do not feel obliged." Her tone was ice-cold in spite of the heat.

He stared at her, stunned and expressionless, not unlike the day he was doused with water from her balcony. "What on earth are you talking about?"

"Finally, we have some honesty. You said you wanted to talk with me some, and I actually believed you. But it seems you are not given to talking, and my talking is interrupting your contemplations. So, let's continue with this newfound honesty; give this the rating of a bad idea and abandon it while we are ahead." She was hot and bothered, and turned impatiently to leave. She had actually taken a full dozen steps before he strode after her and stood in her path.

"I'm sorry. You are annoyed."

"Very perceptive." She tried to step around him, but he sidestepped and blocked her way.

"Maggie, I'm sorry. Please. I'm not good at this. It has been a while. Can we just find some shade? I would rather sit."

She closed her eyes and took a deep breath. She didn't find nine-year-olds this trying. She nodded. They sat in the shade of a gum tree, Maggie leaning up against its pale trunk. She held a cluster of gumnuts, picking them off, twirling them in her fingers and flicking them away.

He looked contrite. "I'm sorry. I was rude. You were right to call me on it."

Maggie flicked another gumnut and made no attempt to respond. She had done her bit, and her enthusiasm for this outing had completely evaporated. It was time for him to do some work towards this. Whatever "this" was.

McCray sighed and looked up into the long white branches of the gum tree. "When I am around you I find my thoughts flow where they have been suffering a great deal of congestion. I had not even realised it, but I was taking advantage of that unobstructed stream."

"I assume that is an attempt at flattery. I find you have the opposite effect on me." She really had come prepared to be amiable, but he just seemed to bring out the worst in her.

"I am being quite sincere. I have clarity on some things I have been mulling over quite repetitively."

Sammy was wrong. She didn't need to know him better at all. Everything she knew about him at this moment was quite sufficient. "Well, I suppose that is pleasant for you, knowing I am some sort of intellectual purgative. Doesn't do much for my sense of feeling attended to though."

He considered her for a moment. Really? Did everything need to be a wrestling match? He resisted the urge to stand to his feet and bid her good day. Was he wrong about this? Where was the music he had sensed as she floated up those stairs, or at dinner when she glowed like an angel, or as they glided in a waltz around the library? Was that really only a week ago? He searched her face, intensely looking for it. Maggie suddenly felt the need to glance away. There: it was just there hovering under the surface, almost as if it was fighting for air. In the transparency of that moment, he suddenly recognised this music was a fragile thing. And he had an overwhelming desire to protect and care for it so he would never lose the music again.

"Maggie, it seems that even if I am skilled in the logic of Chess, I lack finesse in other matters that are important to me. And although you have the gift of telling mysterious stories of adventure to your students, you show a surprising lack of curiosity regarding the dilemmas of real life. Is this another of your incongruencies, intended to throw me off balance?"

"I hardly think your lack of finesse is in any way related to the level of my curiosity. The two are completely unconnected and that you might suggest they are in some way dependent on your sense of balance is quite unnecessary. Flattery yet again."

"There – see? I am charged with imprudent behaviour once more. In reality, I am floundering for a way to tell you the essence of the conversation I had with your father."

"Strictly speaking, Sammy is my uncle."

"Strictly speaking, he could not be more paternal. I trust I do as well for our daughter."

Maggie glared at him horrified, and then burst out laughing. "Oh, you are completely fearless. I would not have believed it possible for a man to say something like that before he has even dared to ask a lady out."

He smiled. "Now that *was* intended to flatter. I might as well submit to the crime I have already been convicted of."

Sammy's words came rushing back: "*...you've drawn and quartered him without so much as a pause...*" Really? Was she so unfair? She was determined to prove she could be fair, regardless of how ridiculous it was. "Then I suppose, I am obliged to hear you out. And you are quite wrong about my curiosity, but prudence demands a level of discrete restraint, however intense my inquisitive impulses."

He breathed out slowly; relieved she had resumed her position on the fencing-piste, willing to dance along the playing-field, back and forth, to cross swords and parry again. He relaxed just a little. "Well then, strictly speaking, I have been given the go-ahead by your father-uncle, to seek your consent, as it is my hope to pursue a courtship with you."

Maggie looked at him nonplussed and said nothing, brushing ants off her skirt. He could have been ordering hessian bags from the general store. It held nothing of the romance she perhaps may have imagined such a moment could hold... should have held. It occurred to her momentarily, the gesture was a spear thrown into the flank of her Minotaur: reality destroying the myth. It was not a fatal blow by any means and effectively it just made the Minotaur very mad. She flicked another gumnut out into the sunlight and waited, her pride writhing. But McCray evidently had nothing much to add. He didn't even look at her. Finally, she said, rather curtly, "Well then. Strictly speaking, you have permission to ask a question. Do you think it likely you will ever ask that question?"

He looked at her then and measured his words. He didn't know how to take her sometimes. Courting Ann was never like this; she made it so simple by conforming to every traditional gesture. Maggie was determined to be contrary. "I thought I might. In fact, I have considered 'when' and 'where' and 'how'. I have wondered what would appeal to you most. You see, Miss Wick, I have never dared to assume your answer is necessarily going to be the one I so desperately want to hear. And I do like to give myself the best chances of success."

He was certainly straightforward, perhaps another plunging of the spear. But this time she smiled as she realised the theme of incongruency reared up again. "So, you thought that ignoring my attempts at conversation; sitting in the heat under a tree among ants and gumnuts would help load the dice of chance in your favour?"

He laughed. "What can I say? You remind me that I need to navigate very carefully as I am actually sailing uncharted waters. I think to my shame I essentially forgot I had not even had this conversation. You are an enigma to me, Maggie. You are the most comfortable and agitating person I have ever known. I feel like I have known you forever, and then I find you are a complete conundrum to me. I don't understand how you cannot see I am completely bewitched by you, and yet it seems I only have the effect of causing you the greatest irritation. What am I to do?"

She looked into his eyes and was surprised by the frank dilemma she saw held there. She believed he had been entirely honest. "I would not fear too much. It seems whatever you and Sammy spoke of, he is of the most sympathetic mind towards you. He has warned me most severely to give myself a chance to learn your character and not to judge too swiftly, a failing I am apparently prone to. So, all in all, I think your chances of a positive response to such a question are fairly good. Not guaranteed, but good."

His eyes smiled. "Then, it appears it would be expedient not to delay such a question any longer. Perhaps I was tempted to assume I need not ask it of you at all." He leant forward, filling her vision. "Maggie Wick, would you allow me to show you my character? I want you to see me, strengths and flaws, and me to see you… to continue to shed light on the most intriguing person I have yet encountered. Will you allow me to court you?"

She paused, staring at his eyes and then his lips, deliberately drawing out the moment. She knew she would say yes, just as she was sure he knew that too. She had a moment of depravity where she wanted to knock his knees out from under him, to exert her power and leave him flattened. But as she pictured him buckled in pain, an intense ache rose in her throat and she felt herself reach out to protect him. She lifted her finger and silenced him. "Oh Duncan, I'm not sure this is a good idea. I don't want to hurt you."

"Why do you assume you will?"

"You see what we are like! No one… I mean I *never* speak my mind with anyone like I do with you. How can this be a healthy way to determine if…"? She couldn't help it, "… if I will be a suitable mother for your daughter?"

"*Our* daughter," he corrected, and then searched her sober eyes. Yes, she was capable of a great deal of hurt, as was he. He knew. "Yes, I believe you are right. Hurt comes with the territory. But in the discovering, we will also learn to soothe those hurts. Otherwise, the rest will never come to be and then sadly…" and he added with a glint of fun in his eye… "I will never get to meet our daughter. Still, let's not jump ahead."

"It was not me who jumped ahead by bringing that up."

"And?" He reached out and placed his hand over hers. "Your answer? You demand I ask a question but then leave me hanging without an answer…"

"My answer is… yes. But don't bl…" He gently smothered the rest of her words with the back of his hand.

"No qualifiers. That is all I need just now."

❧ • ❧

He leaned back and stretched out his long legs. She said yes. He let out a sigh. Had he been holding his breath? This marked the passing of a momentous landmark and he felt immense relief as if someone had taken a block and tackle and lifted the most incredible weight off his chest. He propped himself on his elbow and closed his eyes in the lazy warmth of the afternoon. His brow creased slightly in a frown.

Out of the shrubbery rang the unremarkable tones of a peewee duet, and Maggie felt her senses sway with the timing of their song. It may not be pretty or melodious, and even the rhythm was mostly off-beat. It surprised her how normal this birdsong sounded. It occurred to her that she was embarking on an endeavour to see if she too could sing with another. Duncan looked over and said, "Would you like some afternoon tea? It is too warm to walk home without some refreshment." She looked puzzled as he sat up and Tom emerged from the bushland with a loaded picnic basket.

Maggie smiled at Tom as his eyes twinkled at her. "I hope you were paid handsomely for rendering this service?" she said to him.

He shrugged and then quickly nodded as McCray looked at him twice. "Yes Miss Maggie, the Captain gave me two pennies and a pocket-knife."

Duncan shrugged. "He drove a hard bargain."

"And you have delivered it at the perfect time. Thank you, Tom. Your shadowing skills are doing you well." She blushed a little at the thought they had an audience. "Yes, you may have a muffin. I'm sure Lonnie put in an extra one." Maggie passed Tom a muffin and he scampered into the shadows and disappeared.

Maggie poured a drink for them both and offered a selection of oatmeal biscuits and cakes. "So, would you mind if I asked you something to mollify my restless curiosity?"

He studied the mug in his hand as he again stretched out. He nodded. "Okay."

Maggie said, "You mentioned you had things you were thinking about. What kind of thoughts congests the mind of a station manager? What causes the Black King of Logic to ponder so deeply over his Kingdom?"

He considered his muffin. He had read her correctly – of course, she would ask, but how much real-life was he actually willing to disclose? "The position of his Queen – his most valuable asset. The safety of his people, even the pawns – those whom some players see as dispensable." Just by speaking it out, the stream began to flow again, smooth ripples of fluid thought. "And then the resources of the Kingdom, in this case – cattle. We've had ten more head go this week – that's nigh fifty in just over a month. That's a lot of money with the market the way it is. Henderson hasn't got back to me, and the constables haven't come out to file a report. It is the weirdest thing. Even Blondie says he can't work out what's happened, and that alone is particularly disturbing because I've seen that man track ghosts. I can't discount the thought he may be involved in a duffing ring."

Maggie looked shocked. "Blondie? He stuck by Henderson when others left. You can't seriously thi…"

He looked at her sharply and cut her off. "You asked what I thought. I have been trying to find an explanation; this is something I have to consider." He leaned back on his elbow and said nothing for a while. It felt significant that he could be honest. "Water's an issue, just as always; I'm costing up more wind-mills to access water further out. Then, on top of that, I found in the mail… brought in by the preacher today, the follow-up letter that confirms that the teacher of our school has been put on an inspector's list." Maggie sat upright, her mouth opened, but no sound came forth. "It's not a routine inspection, but rather an investigation of our particular arrangement. This is not the best way to tell her I'm sure, and I'm not even certain what the implications are with the Board of General Education. I don't believe they have any grounds to conduct an investigation at all, unless it is to verify the criteria to resume our funding. Also, my head-stockman is considering leaving given the tone of the district, and that would wipe out half the school enrolments. That would also put a massive hole in my experienced station-hands because Blondie and a couple of others would probably go with him. I've had to put my son's nanny on a good behaviour warning: I found her paralytic from intoxication late last Wednesday night. Normally I would sack someone immediately for that – but it *was* Thelma's night off, and Alex didn't see anything. In loyalty to Ann, it didn't seem right. And then…"

Her head was spinning. "There's more?"

"Well, just one thing. My groundsman: he said that should I ever put a step wrong with his daughter he would personally take a shotgun to me, and willingly go to the gallows for it." He looked at Maggie gravely and said, "I remembered what you said. I checked under the sideboard – there really is a shotgun there. I can't help but think twice when Sammy is pouring drinks. Oh, but in the end, he did say it would never come to that because Lonnie would have me poisoned and buried before he could get to me anyway."

She grimaced. "My family is loyal… to a fault." She paused. "Sammy really said that? He was so determined I would not misjudge you, yet he said that?"

He smirked. "I do not doubt his sincerity for a moment. You seem to attract intense devotion, Maggie."

Maggie stared at him. She said nothing for a long time. She cringed inside over her petulant demands for attention. "Yet in all of this, you would plan a picnic for me? Now I am flattered."

"And I am relieved. I was not so sure of my hand. You are not so bad at playing poker yourself Miss Wick."

"I am a terrible poker player." She reached over to pack away the biscuits from a trail of ants gathering around the basket. "You, however, are a master. Who would even know all that is going on? And the Black King, how does he fare? Does the game go well for him?"

"Just picking his next move."

"But you are not intimidated?"

He looked right into her heart and he thought for a moment his chest would explode from the pressure it felt there. He stood to his feet, willing himself to pick up the basket. He did not take his eyes from her gaze. "Intimidation can have its uses it seems. I have an intense desire to jump ahead, but a particular conversation with Sammy suggests that would be stupidity. I am too young to die so I must get you back to the homestead."

She took his hand and stood to her feet. "And I'm too fragile to be orphaned twice in a lifetime."

He smiled. "Fragile? Maggie, really?"

"Yes, their acts of retribution would mean the gallows for both of them, so I feel a level of responsibility to ensure they have no cause to take you out."

"See – you don't doubt their sincerity either."

"I am their only child," she said lightly with a shrug.

They walked back along the track, Maggie's mind spinning with the things she had been told. Duncan looked at her. "Now I see *you* are distracted."

"I know I asked about your thoughts, and I know you did not tell me to cause me to worry. I also know they are not my concerns... well, the school being the exception of course. But I really want to understand. Is this a usual week in the life of Duncan McCray? Is all this just the random busyness of station life, or is there any connection between these things? How do you process such dilemmas? Leon never shared these aspects of his life with me. Either he had no depth of thought – and that is a real possibility, or he considered it male-territory that I was not permitted to trespass, which is far more likely. Yet I want to appreciate the position you are in. Is this crossing the boundaries of schoolteacher – as friend, even a courted one? Can I even want this?"

He stopped and put down the basket. He turned to her and lifted her chin. "Maggie Wick, one day you will be my wife. Please understand this is my intention. If you have the slightest inkling you want anything else, then you had better run for the hills, because if you stay I *will* marry you. To that end, schoolteacher or friend, please – get inside my head. You are already in my heart. I want you to know me... more than anything." He leant down and kissed her lightly on her forehead and forced himself to pull away. "Almost anything," he whispered.

Maggie closed her eyes and evened her breathing. "Minotaur," she said quietly.

Duncan looked at her and for a split second wondered if he had been too bold and said too much.

She took his hand and studied the calluses across his palm. "You have been progressively attacking my Minotaur, the monster of Greek Mythology. I believe, Sir Theseus, that probably was its fatal blow. There can be no mystery left when you expose your intentions like that." She tilted her head and looked into the deep blue colour of the summer sky. "Wow. Am I really free from its tyranny?" She laughed lightly at the clouds. "Right now, I have no fear of being torn apart or dismembered; sacrificed to serve some cause; or squeezed into some mould I do not fit. If you truly live up to that declaration Theseus, I could seriously consider being your wife."

"How can I want you to fit a shape that is not you? It is *you* who has me cowering out of respect for your parents."

"Hmm, we will see. I know your intentions; you have made them clear. And I must say, it smacked... just a little, of a dare. Well, the judge and jury will be presented with evidence, and at some point, a deliberation will be required. I am very curious to see if you *can* live up to it."

"I am on trial? I think of courtship as a dance – learning to move to music, like in the library… finding the rhythm and timing of the other. Not a *court*room!"

She laughed. "It did seem a little apostate of me, to hold a heathen metaphor of romance based on fickle Greek gods and monsters requiring sacrifice. Yes, I really do need different imagery. Right here, you have presented me with some genuine possibilities: dance, duet, courtroom trial…"

They walked on for a while, their thoughts filling the silence between the rhythms of their steps. "Duncan, what is this talk about Takings? Is Jones seriously thinking of leaving? He's been here forever; Henderson's Gap is his home."

He said nothing for a while. "Wouldn't worry too much about it. I can't see these Removal Laws will have much impact here. What these people call 'Takings', others call 'Stealing'. That's a tad sensationalised. The laws are mostly protective measures used to remove loitering Blacks unable to work, or the old and indigent – those who can't look after themselves. This area is not impoverished like other places; it can hardly be applied here. Henderson has very generous views towards locals."

"Olivia was worried about it. Her family is here."

"People hear stories, and the stories are not always helpful or true."

"But she said people were saying the Jones' kids should be included. Priscilla is not yet twelve: she is still a child. Surely they would never take a child from their family?"

"She's enrolled in school. It doesn't apply. Be reassured, the policy is used to ensure kids attend school where they wouldn't normally get that opportunity. Like I said – Jones' mob, they're already enrolled. That's why they started the school in the first place. There's no reason for him to go. I've told him that."

17.

Life did find a new rhythm: school days, Wednesday nights, Friday afternoon meetings… and sometimes a weekend excursion on the river or a horse ride to the back paddocks. Terry's feathers grew white – and his crest glowed a sulphur-yellow. He squawked a loud herald whenever the Captain came to class, even when he slipped a slice of dried apple onto his perch. It seemed the bird refused to consider him anything but an intrusion. A new family with three school-aged children moved onto the neighbouring property. They were quickly enrolled.

Maggie routinely reviewed each school week with McCray on Friday afternoons. Another letter from the Board of General Education presented itself on McCray's desk, offering an opportunity to alleviate their concerns before they proceeded with the formal investigation. Exactly what concerns seemed a little vague, but Maggie helped draft another report, updating the status of the school, facilities, enrolments and a request for funding to be resumed on the basis all criteria were being met according to the guidelines.

Maggie spoke with Jones about starting a regular church meeting, having get-togethers a little more formally than discussions around his fire-hearth. Jones hesitated. He had his own ideas about what "meeting together" meant according to Scripture's admonition not to neglect this important means of encouragement. Finally, he conceded one did not preclude the other and they made a plan to invite neighbouring families for a Sunday service every fortnight.

Yes, life was operating at a pleasant tempo. Wednesday evenings were the highlight of Maggie's week. Sometimes the chessboard stood unattended, sometimes not. One evening Duncan ushered Maggie into the dining room to see Sammy and Lonnie had been invited to dinner. They sat dressed in their best clothes, like stuffed pigs on a spit, awfully uncomfortable to be sitting instead of serving. But the Captain insisted it was their night off and made every effort to help them relax. "Please, allow me," and he went and served the meal he had ordered Lonnie to prepare the day before.

Lonnie grumbled in Mandarin as they filled their plates. Was there any point in having to work twice as hard one day, to be invited out to dinner the next? Maggie clearly understood the injustice she felt. Sammy made the amused comment, "At least we know the food is good." Alex stared at Lonnie wide-eyed. He had never seen her sitting at the dining table. Nor had he seen her dressed in her brightly embroidered Chinese glad-rags; nor heard her speak Mandarin so emphatically.

When they had finished their meal, Lonnie got up and cleared the table, ignoring Maggie's protests. "Sammy – pour drinks," she instructed and left. Duncan eyed the drink pouring procedure carefully as Sammy bent down to fix his boot a number of times fiddled with something under the sideboard.

Maggie reached over and quietly reassured him, "He's just teasing."

"All in devotion to you Maggie."

Lonnie appeared with a lemon pie. When the Captain raised his brows, Lonnie huffed unjustly. "Don't think I go to dinner with my daughter's beau and not bring *somethink* for dessert."

With one look at Lonnie, Duncan resigned himself to a horrible death by poisoning, if this was her intent. At least it would be a delicious demise.

When Sammy and Lonnie retired to their quarters and after Alex was settled in bed, Duncan came down to the library and poured himself a drink, stronger than limewater. He sat on the chesterfield and gazed at the chessboard. "Maggie, just so you know, you never had a hope of being dull and uninteresting. 'Bland' is not your heritage.

She quietly looked into his eyes. "Thank you for inviting them," she said. She wasn't sure how to explain how touched she was by such a generous gesture. To be raised by a Chinese woman was a social disgrace. "Leon's family was never willing to acknowledge Lonnie. They were satisfied with Aunt

Winifred – her pedigree and money, her strong political contacts, and social standing made her acceptable. But it seemed they had made a private pact that my life didn't start until I turned twelve and arrived at Aunt Winifred's. Sammy is Winifred's brother, but that never counted for anything. Two strong people who married in different directions. Sammy warned me, but I cried and cried the first time I really understood Lonnie was not considered as good as them." Maggie's eye's filled with tears. "In the end, I gave in to them. In town, they arrest people for loitering with Chinese! I bought into the lie. I didn't write... at least not often; I didn't visit; and I didn't let anyone know my mother was a Chong. She disappeared from my history. How could I do that?" It was her darkest secret: her most humiliating failure. "And yet when I came back Lonnie never mentioned it. She never judged my neglect of her. She just made me a cup of tea as if I'd been away for the weekend." Shame filled her with grief.

"Lonnie often talked about 'her girl". But I sort of assumed her *girl* was about twelve years old, with pigtails like her mother."

"That was me when I left. How could I be ashamed of someone who loved me so well? Even when she..." Emotion flared up behind Maggie's eyes glistening as tears.

"I guess that makes it love," he said softly. "I know Lonnie is not your birth-mother, but your connection with her is just as strong." Then he chuckled. "Sammy is a tough man to have two such women in his life and still be sane."

"See that? This is what I find most curious. Out there, Chow, Chong, Chink is a disease. Probably something even far more deep-seated – a moral impairment beyond curable. But you don't look at her that way. Lonnie might annoy you, but that is because she can be annoying, not because she is Chinese. There is a big difference, and it is very unusual Mr McCray. But you don't seem to want to offer an explanation outside being some sort of celestial saint, which I don't actually believe to be the case."

He took another drink and shrugged. "Saintly has worked so far, but it seems you are onto me. I am found out. Celestial, I am not." He sat grinning at her for a while, teasing her with his disinclination to say anything more. But by virtue of his own declaration he had to offer something more substantial. How else could she see him – strengths and flaws? He got up and went over to the bookcase. He selected a volume with a latch and laid it on the lounge. "There really is no mystery. This is one of my diaries. You may open it."

Maggie turned the little key and opened the metal latch. The pages inside had been glued and carved out to create a small box. In the cavity was a collection of strange Asian trinkets. "I was stationed in Hong Kong. I was wounded not long after I arrived so my tour of duty was a rather four-walled experience. The injury was not too serious – although it did leave a half-interesting scar, which I would very much like to show you some time in the future," he added with a sprinkling of mischief. "But it was the reoccurring bouts of Breakbone Fever coupled with Malaria that were not so kind. Because of my rank, I was given private care. I owe my life to a Chinese doctor and his wife who nursed me around the clock. Overall, I stayed with them for months, and by the time I got on top of it, my battalion had returned here. I learnt Mandarin quite well, mainly because I was dying from boredom when everything else could not kill me. I'm pretty sure Lonnie would not be so free with her opinions if she knew." He smiled as the keeper of a grand secret. "By my honour, please don't tell her!"

Maggie blushed. "You understood what she said at dinner?"

He smirked. "And she makes a valid point. But I couldn't serve *my* cooking, so what choice did I have? I must admit Lonnie's venting has given me endless causes for amusement and saved me dozens of times. My favourite was your first day at school after class when she likened your visit as being thrown into a lion's den. I felt so powerful."

She gasped. "You heard that! I was terrified. I remember you made a comment about Chinese tigers. I thought that was so ironic, but you knew!"

"See you weren't the only one who felt at the mercy of big cats. Imagine what I thought when Lonnie started huffing and puffing about Wednesday night dress codes for our chess games. Simple white... I wore simple black. Then there was the horror of a ball gown. I had no idea what to do with that! How could I rise to such a challenge? You had me."

"You cheated! You knew my hand. When you walked in looking so imposing and handsome, I..." Maggie blushed.

"Then there were horse rides and boat excursions. As a source, she proved very reliable."

"I change my accusation from celestial to conniving. Don't you feel any shame?"

"No, not really. You had me bouncing all over the place like a grasshopper. I had to use what was at my disposal."

"But to enlist my family without their knowing seems... calculated, merciless."

"Oh, Sammy knows. He volunteered observations dozens of times that were very timely."

"Sammy! Unbelievable. I *will* take this up with him. If that means Lonnie finds out you are secretly more conversant in Mandarin than myself, I am not responsible." She wondered why she didn't feel annoyed. Perhaps it was seeing his frank desire to gain her parents' approval at dinner, which would have been just as convincing if he had been a nervous young suitor dining at the halls of Fairfield.

She returned her focus to what she held in her hand. She lifted the items from the trinket-box book: a jade pendant on a cord; a fragment of rice-parchment with ink writing; a silk ribbon; a shard of fine pottery; a piece of soft leather; a string of glass beads; a little cloth sack of rice grain; ivory chopsticks; and a miniature wooden figurine. She held each curiosity, intrigued, wondering at this unique way of journaling experiences. Each had a story and he quietly told her some of them.

She reverently returned the items, closed the book and snapped shut the latch. Somehow his private encounter with Chinese life, even while he was sick and confined, was loaded with insight. She had loved just one person, however poorly, but it seemed he loved the culture.

When Maggie made the observation that his appreciation of Chinese society had not successfully neutralised Lonnie's persisting disfavour, he shrugged. "You said yourself, Chinese are by nature loyal to a fault. Lonnie is Henderson-loyal. Perhaps Henderson became her family because, in my experience, they are strictly family-loyal. I've seen a lot of them make a bucket-load of money that they would send back home while they lived like paupers. When I came, I upset a lot of 'Henderson' routines. Everything I dared change became a slight against Henderson and a criticism of the way he preferred to do things. Like... well, I had the audacity to move breakfast to half-nine when I come in from the paddocks. I have something to eat when I get up, but by mid-morning I am seriously looking for Lonnie's hash-browns and bacon. She knows I don't loiter on the verandah sipping tea until ten, but she insists that I do... mostly to herself, and mostly in Chinese. Perhaps the time will come when she makes the switch, and the next person will suffer at the hand of McCray routines."

18.

The following Wednesday, Maggie sat staring at the chess pieces. Duncan looked across the chessboard and said; "You know I have you in five moves." She refused to respond but stayed intensely riveted on the board. He got up and walked around the room. "I must admit this third game has lasted far longer than I ever thought possible. You have remarkable stamina, Maggie."

"This is, in fact, our fourth game," she said quietly, otherwise ignoring his jibes. "You might remember we agreed on the best out of five. If you win this our next game will be the tie-breaker…"

He continued lightly, "Come, take a break. Perhaps you will get a moment of clarity and see your way through." He sat down on the chesterfield and studied her furrowed brow.

Without moving she said very quietly and firmly, "No. I will not concede. I will not go out without a fight. And I will not give up until the last move is played."

He considered her. "I think that is fair. It is confirmed beyond doubt: you are not a quitter. But I believe some games are not intended to be won or lost. The value is in the playing."

"So, he tries to distract me with philosophy. It will hardly work."

"So perhaps I can distract you with secrets. Private unspoken secrets…"

She smiled at that and raised her eyebrows but kept looking at the game. "More interesting at least."

He groaned, faking disappointment. "What a pity I have none worthy of telling. Although…" He paused a moment and then plunged ahead, "have I ever told you about Alex's mother – Ann?"

Maggie's body did not move, the chess pieces no longer in focus. She tilted her face slowly towards Duncan who was sitting comfortably on the chesterfield, his legs crossed out in front of him. "Do you *want* to talk about her, or just distract me from retrieving my position from imminent danger?"

"Neither. I am pining from neglect and realised I have to pull something significant from my bag to get a little focused attention."

She got up from the table and sat down beside him. "Well, I think it has worked: you have my attention. The chessboard has waited this many weeks. It can wait for another evening."

"Do you humour me because I desire your attentiveness, or because you are consumed with curiosity regarding the '*other woman*'?"

"Neither. Suddenly chess has little appeal. You sit there baiting me, only to find you have been thinking of another. I am female enough to jealously regard your exclusive admiration."

He rubbed his chin. "I hadn't thought of that. Which puts me in an awkward position, because now that I have brought it up, I suspect it will not go away without talking about it."

"Duncan, you don't have to. You know that."

"Hmm. I think I do."

"Well, now you mention it, my curiosity has been given a lot of scrutiny since coming to Henderson's Gap." Her voice softened. "You loved her very much didn't you?"

He stood up and pulled out a little drawer in the side of the chess table. He drew out a small frame with a photographic portrait of an attractive woman with a languid smile. He handed it to Maggie. Suddenly this indistinct figure had an identity. She was a real person. Tangible. Ann. Maggie's hand trembled as she took the frame. "She looks so fragile."

"She was, in her way. And kind. She was also reflective. I remember you said that of Alex once. He has a lot of his mother's nature."

Alex's mother. Maggie was shocked to realise they had played chess – with all their banter – over the shadow of his wife, her portrait lying face up in the drawer of the table. Was it possible the man was still in love? Maggie put the portrait down and got up to walk around. Emotions tumbled to the surface that she didn't recognise. She wasn't sure where to look. "What was she like?"

"I will not lie. My new bride was something of a remarkable treasure. Ann had the sweetest nature; her family was positioned; she was attentive and lovely. At that time, I was blissfully happy."

Maggie dared to look at his eyes and saw the tender feelings that had surfaced, stirred by her memory. As she turned away, his eyes darkened with a profound sadness, his brow furrowed deeply. Maggie stood there, staring out the window into the night. So, his Ann had been everything to him, everything she was not. Maggie was sufficiently self-aware to know she was not fragile or compliant or sweet or attentive or… positioned. It was like a maze of menace quickly tangled up to hedge her in. She didn't know which way to turn.

"We had our plans for starting a family. On a trajectory of success and ambition, everything was on track." He had paused, silent and grim. Maggie turned and saw he had closed his eyes and she noticed the pained pursed line of his lips, reminiscent of the man she first met standing behind his desk. He took a breath and made himself continue.

"Then, somewhere, at some point, it was like something… everything inside her crumbled… and I have no idea what actually happened. Alex's birth was hard and it seemed Ann never recovered… herself.

Thelma raised Alex from the start. When he was about eight months old there was a Barracks Picnic Day. It was a different sort of outing and Ann really didn't want to go, but I insisted. I thought it would help for her to have an outing. She seemed to cheer up some, and I felt justified in my pushing. The thought of a ride in the boats along the river seemed to please her. It was such a relief. I thought we would..." He stopped, his face pale. "When they pushed out from the bank she stood up. Suddenly she fell overboard and never resurfaced. The officer in the boat had no indication anything was amiss. She didn't jump. He said she looked at him and smiled and then seemed to lose her balance and fall backwards, but she didn't appear to struggle either. He said he thought she was just being plucky – going into the water like that... and it took him a while to realise she wasn't coming up. There were dozens from the regiment in the water but it still took us ages to find her. She was downriver some distance. There was nothing we could do. We don't know if it was a terrible accident or she meant to. We went with the terrible accident."

The room went quiet. The candles seemed to flicker wanly. Duncan sat staring blankly at the board of chess pieces. He stood up abruptly and paced around the room. "Damn it!" and he swore fiercely under his breath. "One moment, life is everything I could want: I win at everything I put my hand to..." He waved at the chessboard, "...and then in one fell swoop, I have nothing." He leant over the game-table and with a dramatic swipe of his forearm, he swept all the pieces onto the chesterfield lounge. They lay littered like bodies on a conquered battlefield. Maggie stared at their symbolic downfall. She didn't register then, that their game was decimated. All she could see was the transparent failure burning in his eyes.

"You have Alex."

"Yes. That is all. He is absolutely all I have. I couldn't stand to be away from him. I discharged and took this job. It seemed here I might be the parent I wasn't while Ann was alive... *barely* alive. And so, you see Maggie, I do know how to lose, and I don't like it. Coming here was about repairing and regaining control. Which seemed to be working quite well until one Tuesday morning someone burst into the Library with a breakfast tray and tossed its contents all over the floor."

The way he said it, Maggie was not sure whether he resented her intrusion on his life or not. It was bizarre. He had just trusted her with his most intimate tragedy, and she knew she should be honoured by the confidence, yet she felt... she felt... she didn't know how she felt at all. She looked at the clock on the mantle. It was not yet nine. "I'm sorry, it is really late. I think I will retire." And before he could respond she fled the room and ran to her quarters.

∾•∿

Maggie half expected Duncan to follow her that night. He didn't. Then she thought it likely he would come to the classroom the next day. He didn't. By Thursday evening she was resigned that he might never want to see her again; her panicky exit being an offence too great to endure. Just like Hastings of Fairfield. She ploughed through the lessons on Friday with a headache pounding at her temples. She sent a message to Lonnie at the big house, asking her to deliver an apology for her Friday school meeting. She was unwell.

There was a knock at the lattice door. Maggie groaned and rolled over. "Lonnie, please tell me you brought some chicken soup. My head is thumping!"

There was a pause before the door opened. "Yes, I have brought soup. I guess Lonnie is right: her soup is the best prescription under these circumstances." Duncan's voice was deep and soft and concerned.

Maggie cringed. She didn't want to see him, and she certainly didn't want him to see her like this. She sat up in bed and pulled a shawl around her shoulders. Her eyes were red from crying and her hair tousled. Duncan removed the petticoats that hung over the arms of a chair and dragged it up beside the bed. Without speaking he positioned a tray and poured the jar of soup into a bowl. He sat down and said nothing. She reluctantly took up her spoon. She had not eaten all day, but she doubted even Lonnie's soup could make her feel better. Her eyes welled up again, and she blew her nose on the serviette folded on her tray.

She dared to look at him. He sat stiff like a fire-poker, his mouth grim and his brow creased. She finished the soup. They said nothing for a long time. The throbbing in her head eased to a dull ache. A fleeting thought crossed her mind. She should ask Lonnie how she prepared the chicken stock. She was sure there was more than White Willowbark powder in the recipe. He removed the tray wordlessly and placed it on the floor beside him.

He knew he had to say something, but he struggled to know how to start. Would it mean he would lose here as well? "Is it just your head that aches?"

Maggie slid down between the sheets, pulling the covers up close to her chin. She rolled on her side, her tears wetting the pillowcase as they spilled over when she blinked. She couldn't speak. How could he know every part of her body was screaming in pain trying to regain some sort of equilibrium? How could he ever comprehend how much this hurt?

Finally, he took a deep breath, bracing himself as he did before plunging into an active war-front. "Maggie, I wanted you to understand my relationship with Ann because she is, and will always be, Alex's mother. She *was* my wife."

The tears flowed again, and it was as if they released some of the agony Maggie felt push to the surface over the last two days. Her breath came in shuddering gasps. "She was everything I am not. You could not pick two more different women if you scoured the earth."

His brow creased just a little more. "Apparently not as different as I thought. Both women with an inclination for tears."

"I can never be Ann for you. How could anyone live up to such an image? It is a preposterous expectation! What makes you think this could ever be good, for you… or Alex?" And a fresh flow of tears ran into her pillow.

"I never said I wanted you to be Ann! Do you think you are a retrieval plan for what I lost? Is that what you think?" His voice had the edge of anger to it.

It held enough sharpness to make Maggie pause and look directly at him through red-rimmed eyes. She sat up. "You are angry at me? How is this my fault? I am not Ann – I am just me… but apparently, that is not who you want. Am I to blame because I am not pretty or compliant, or sweet and gentle? No! I am not any of those things. I wilfully speak my mind, and I ride horses, and row boats on rivers!" Duncan stared at her. "And to think you would hold her photograph in the drawer of the very table where we played chess while you "court" *me*… casting a shadow on every move. It is evident you wish with every fibre of your being it were she and not I, who sat playing white. You love her still! A woman knows the look of a man in love. The way you looked at her photograph... my goodness! Five years is not long to grieve the love of a lifetime." The fact he was capable of such devotion spun in her mind. He was right. It was not just her head that hurt. It was her heart. She had found her Theseus, but he belonged to another.

Duncan stared into the paintwork on the wall across her bed. His fixed gaze becoming more and more intense. Suddenly he got up and walked out. He didn't close the door to her room, and she could hear him pacing up and down, his hard boots clipping against the boards on the verandah. He seemed to go and on. Finally, he came back inside. He stood at the end of her bed. Tears rolled down her cheeks. Eventually, he sat down again.

"One – you are upset by this and that gives me hope. Sometimes it feels like you are above loving me Maggie. But this distresses you and that means something." He took a breath. "Two – Ann was not without her flaws. But she was a good person, and I will always honour her as Alex's mother." He reached out and took her hand. "Three – the table where I kept the photograph was given to us as a wedding present. It had been in her family for a long time. I always found that ironic, given that Ann did not even like chess. After the funeral, I offered to return it to her father because of its history. They asked that it be kept for Alex. It is Alex's table and I had his permission to play our games on it. That is why the photograph is kept there; he wanted it there. He has another one in his room." He traced her hand with his finger, slowly, thoughtfully. "Four – yes, you speak your mind, and yes, you are different to Ann. But I didn't have to scour the earth, because *you* found me, Maggie Wick. I didn't go looking for this. Who would ever have thought Henderson's Gap would turn up something as remarkable as you? Not in a million years would I have thought it possible. That was one of the reasons I came here. I didn't *just* come here to parent. I came here to hide." He lifted her hand to his lips and kissed the back of her hand. "Five – whether you like it or not: Ann is a reality of my past. But you are all I see in my present and my future. Please, Maggie. You have to hear me: I don't love her still. She is gone."

"One question?" He nodded and she looked up at him and blew her nose. "Do you think I am pretty?" She hic-upped and blew her nose again.

He looked at her dishevelled hair, blotchy skin, red nose and swollen eyes. "You have no mercy woman! You lay before me, miserable and crushed… or you stand in the stairwell dressed like an angel… or you glide on the water pondering the mysteries of life… or you ride like a maniac and fear starts strangling me again. You sit on a kitchen stool as if it is in a banquet hall or down by the riverbank as if it is a cathedral. You laugh and my senses spin... you reach out to tuck a shawl under Alex's chin and my world stops moving. The puzzle keeps getting more and more complex. I am no closer to solving this enigma who is before me, than at the beginning. I have no recollection of anyone so beautiful."

"But you did not say pretty..."

He knew he could be in trouble, but he would not disregard what he knew. He reached into his pocket and passed her his kerchief. He spoke softly, soothing her tears with the caress of a man in love. "I would not call this your best pretty-day. Wednesday night was pretty until you left me on an emotional barge set adrift without an anchor. I have needed to find what it is that anchors me. I could not... would not come here until I knew. I cannot be my own anchor, because whether I like it or not, I am mortal, as are you. Mortal cannot anchor mortal. A boat cannot moor another boat. If I am anchored securely, I'm not shattered on the rocks when the storms come." He swallowed hard. He went and poured himself a drink from the jug on her washstand. "You probably think this has nothing to do with 'pretty'. But it does. I am not here just because you are pretty, or compliant, or even comfortable Maggie. I am here because I love you. There is a love that anchors me that reaches beyond mortality. Pretty is not permanent – yet you seem comfortable in it and have more moments than most. But beautiful... *that*, my lovely

Maggie Wick, *that* you do with remarkable consistency."

She had to ask. "And Ann?"

"I will say it and then I will not speak of it again. Ann had pretty days too. But she was also sad; and in the end, she hardly had the capacity to have any more moments that could be called pretty. That was heart-breaking. And it took me a long time to understand it was her heart that was broken too, not just mine."

19.

A serious-looking man in a high-necked cravat stood in the library with three assistants, identically dressed: mindless minions. "McCray, I'm sure you understand the jurisdiction that requires us to investigate this thoroughly. I have been authorised to see this matter attended to in the swiftest and most efficient manner."

McCray considered him evenly. "Four men to do the work of one is hardly my view of efficient. Nevertheless, gentlemen, I assure you of our cooperation to see this matter resolved promptly. We would not wish to tax the resources of a Board that haggles over the meagre wage of a teacher, yet will send an entire committee to solve the problem of an outback schoolyard."

"The sarcasm is quite unnecessary."

"Your presence here is quite unnecessary. Your attention to detail is commendable, but the questions you raise were all addressed in numerous letters sent to your office."

"Obviously they were not sufficiently addressed. There are inconsistencies: the detail you commend us on was lacking in your reports."

"Well Gentlemen, proceed. All the documents you need are in the boxes in the dining room. I know you will be anxious to begin. You will excuse me; I have a Station to run. Miss Wick will be available after classes this afternoon." He said it with a neutral smile, his poker-instincts on high alert. What were they playing at? He knew his attention to detail had not been passed over. Not this time.

"No need. We will be inspecting the school; we can see her then."

"To disrupt lessons is not required. I have documented my reports of regular inspections of the school during its operation. I reiterate: our records are in the dining room. When you speak with Miss Wick this afternoon you can clarify your concerns." He sat down at his desk and proceeded to peruse his ledger, setting about his work without any further reference to them. They looked at each other and made their way to the door."

❧•❧

Maggie was sitting at her desk going over some copy-work when Terry screamed his alert. Lonnie appeared at the door and Maggie quickly went to see what unusual event would bring her to the schoolhouse. She said something quickly in Mandarin and handed her a sheet of paper.

Maggie took it back to her desk and read it through twice. She quietly called Priscilla and Tom to her desk. "I'm going to ask you to do something. It may not make sense, but your Dad has some concerns and he has asked you to do exactly what I say. Take your brother and sisters and go into the scrub. Tom, you are to make sure you all hide in the shadows. He said you would understand. When we hang a towel on the tank-stand it is safe to come back. Don't go home and don't go to the camp. If anyone finds you or tries to pick you up, and you can't get away, tell them you are working on a school project – make sure they understand you are enrolled in school. If you need to stay out overnight, we will leave some things out by the log behind the schoolhouse. You will be okay. Stick together."

Priscilla went pale – her dark skin draining of colour. "Miss, do you think this is a... a Taking?"

"I don't know. I *do* know you are clever, and you know the bush. Your Dad thinks this is best."

Just then two shotgun blasts echoed in the air. Maggie looked into their eyes and pressed her hands against theirs in a gentle grip. "Go now", she whispered. "Go with the protection of God."

She stood up and instructed the class to take out their slates. She wrote on the board a list of exercises and asked how they would start to solve the problems. They were part way through the list when Terry squawked again. The students stopped and gawked.

Sammy was on the verandah with four severe-looking men in long coats. Maggie felt her skin crawl.

They abruptly showed letters of their authority and intent. She ushered them wordlessly inside. "Class – please be up-standing. We have visitors to our classroom." The class scrambled to their feet and offered a mechanical greeting to Mr Kennedy who was in charge. The men checked the roll and noted empty seats. Maggie explained that some students were involved in a special research project. There was a glare and some note-taking. They reviewed the class resources and made more notes. They stood the students, one by one, and checked spelling and number tables. More severe jotting on their notepads.

Gerard raised his hand. The man nodded with a raised brow. "Do you have something to say about the school young man?"

Gerard nodded, and then looked at his slate. He cleared his throat. "My dad says... Ow!" Peter kicked him hard in the shin.

The tension in Maggie's back was twisting tight like screws on a vice. She dropped the blackboard duster hard on the floor.

The man looked at her distracted and then returned back to the student impatiently. "Well, what is it then?"

"My dad says that it's not fair that we have to do book learning with all sorts. Not just Christian people..."

"Do you mean those who are away?" Gerard nodded with a smirk and sniggered when they demanded Maggie explain when the truant students would return. Further notes.

"If my students were truant, I would have no expectation they would return at all. I do, however, believe they will be back in a timely manner. If you would like to wait…" Maggie turned to the class. Perhaps it was better that they were here, and not somewhere else. "We do not have visitors very often; and certainly not from a big community. Gentlemen, it would be delightful if could you explain to the children where you live and what is your favourite aspect of living there?" Kennedy looked startled and then nodded to his assistants. They each answered. One became quite enthralled with the idea of an audience and spoke for a while about trains and libraries. "Well, thank you, that is very interesting. Does anyone have any questions they would like to ask?" The children sat mute. "No? Well, please rub your slates clean and we will proceed with our lessons. It seems our visitors are here to stay." Gerard groaned. His plan to prolong the disruption had backfired with additional Maths calculations. More glares and more notes. Patsy and Alex started to cry. Maggie heard Sammy cock his shotgun and mutter something about snakes.

Kennedy snapped his notepad shut. "I guess not. We will see you at the main house straight after class concludes." They stomped away, fear flowing in their wake. Maggie offered Patsy a handkerchief and gently squeezed Alex's shoulder in reassurance. The rest of the class looked at her white face. Her hands trembled and her palms felt clammy. She relented from the maths problems. "Please understand," she said as she commended them on their respectful behaviour, "what these men need is purely an administration matter. So, let's take our mind off this and read a story… we can resume our exercises later." She opened up their current adventure and soon they were immersed in the exciting escapades of the Arabian Nights.

❧•❧

After class Maggie quietly pushed open the Dining Room door. Arrayed on the table was a mass of documents in piles of varying sizes. The three men sat mute along the table; their hands folded. Mister Kennedy sat grimly at the head of the table. Maggie soberly noted the ratio of investigators to the investigated. She quietly said a prayer: *If my God is with me, merely four men representing the Board of General Education, surely means the ratio is in my favour.* She squared her shoulders and sat down at the table.

Mister Kennedy cleared his throat noisily. He stared at Maggie, like some sort of revolting creature who had crawled out of a swamp. He was uncomfortable with her composure and slammed his pad on the table. She jumped at the sound and she saw a smile light behind his eyes. "It seems Miss Wick, that you fail to understand the seriousness of our visit. You have been reported to The Board of General Education for unethical behaviour and it is our job to verify the quality of the instruction for our students."

"Well then, I'd say the attendance of Mister McCray in this interview will be necessary. Given he has been involved in my appointment here, I insist he hears the nature of your accusations." She didn't wait to be excused but simply stood and walked to the door and was a little surprised to find Sammy at the door, standing against the wall with a shotgun slung over the crook of his arm. She asked him to find Duncan immediately and to have him come to the Dining Room. He nodded and left.

Within minutes she heard the familiar tread of his boots. He nodded curtly at Kennedy as he entered. "Gentlemen?"

"We apologise for the inconvenience. The teacher insists you witness the issues that have been brought to our attention. I personally feel it is an unnecessary intrusion on your time, so you are excused from the need to stay."

He seemed to consider their offer. "I appreciate the respect you give my time, however, I feel a level of responsibility in this matter, as it was Henderson's expressed wish I was to engage the teacher. When the chips are down, as they are now, your concerns are my concerns."

Maggie sat back and considered him. Nothing in his manner indicated they had spent hours head-locked in battles of Chess, bantering across the table, crying over misunderstandings. But this time she didn't fear his apparent lack of attention. *Chips,* he said: *the chips are down.* He was playing Poker. She noticed he didn't sit at the table but went over to the sideboard and poured himself a drink. He knelt down to fiddle with his boot before he stood again and leisurely stood tapping his glass. "Proceed, Gentlemen. Let's get all this ugliness out into the open so we can see what we are dealing with. It is my desire to fix this to your satisfaction, so our funding can be reconnected as soon as possible."

Kennedy coughed and swallowed again. "There are at least five serious complaints that have been brought to our attention."

McCray looked at his drink nonchalantly. "Let's hear them then. So, we don't draw this out unnecessarily, we can deal with the specifics as we go."

Kennedy cleared his throat again. "Firstly, the teacher was employed without due process."

McCray seemed unconcerned and tolerantly said, "That's a serious one Gentlemen. Where do you understand we have neglected the process for starting a provisional school in a remote region?" He knew very well, there were no such requirements. Except for perhaps walking on water. What they had achieved boarded on miraculous.

More coughing. "Character checks, references, qualifications, experience…"

McCray's mouth remained grim. "On which point did we fail?"

"Well to start with, there are no character checks here."

McCray went over to the table and picked up a pile of paper. "Here is the letter of application. Her schooling, experience and previous community endeavours: all listed, with perhaps one omission – she had also been employed as a governess prior to taking this role as well. Jones interviewed her. He was appointed by Henderson to source applicants for the position. Her family has been in the regular employ of Mr Henderson for nigh on twenty-five years, and he personally knows her. This is a reference I could hardly dispute. I have signed these papers of engagement with these conditions, including provisional performance reviews. How can this be lacking to your satisfaction?"

"Are you being impertinent McCray?"

Duncan seemed uninterested in pettiness. "I just want to clarify what we need to do to fix this disgraceful situation, Gentlemen. That is all."

Kennedy coughed again. Two of his skinny sidekicks stood to their feet and left the room. "We will allow that for now. Two. It appears the enrolments were inaccurate, and the school commenced with funding that was fraudulently obtained. Our report will have serious consequences."

"I must assure you this was a grave concern of mine. It appears to be the crux of the matter resulting in the funding being cut off. Once I received the correspondence from your department and recognised they were not as lenient in the ages of students as we originally understood, I went straight to the school. I withdrew Miss Wick from the classroom for an immediate explanation of the situation and the status of enrolments. I have written this in my log, which you have access to. It was determined we needed to remedy the situation with the enrolment of another student over the acceptable age. We were in a position to do this immediately. Since then, we've had three more students enrol. Student numbers are now at fifteen; sixteen if we count the younger girl as she still attends class. And we have another family moving into the district. They have four school-aged children and younger siblings that will be enrolled as they attain age. Can you see any problem with our funding being reconnected now these details have been rectified?"

"You jump ahead of yourself McCray. You have students who should be enrolled in mission schools."

"My understanding of the Board's policy is 'school is school'. Mission options are a matter of convenience rather than a legislated expectation."

"It is rumoured there are blacks at this school – learning alongside whites."

"Rumoured?" It was a question.

"Yes. We heard that…"

"And I heard Australian education wasn't particularly segregationist. It is more a matter of preference."

"Your idealism goes beyond reason. The reality of education throughout the state is they learn better in separate situations."

"And you personally saw students suffering in *this* situation?"

"Some students were away." He checked his notes. "The Jones' family."

"Just to be sure I understand you: there was evidence the other students were disadvantaged?"

"It is not about them – but about those who were not there."

"And I would suggest it is about every student, just as it is about giving every Australian access to education. On this, you cannot fault us."

"We cannot fault you as it cannot be accounted for… conveniently."

"Sammy! Bring Jones in here." There was some scuffling and Jones appeared. Maggie was shocked. He seemed to have aged ten years overnight. "This is my head stockman. His name is Jones: a British name you might note. He is not black. He works with black stockmen and can track as good as any of them.

Whether he gets more sun than the next fellow and tans his hide: that is his business. But I will not have his kids, or mine, disadvantaged because of some rumour children will be educated better sitting beside another. Yes, Gentlemen, my son is also enrolled at the school. So, you can see it would be in *my* interests to ensure the school maintains the highest standards of education. Jones, you are excused."

"McCray, I think you fail to understand the school is under investigation, not the Board of General Education."

Duncan seemed to have lost his patience with the poker game. He poured himself another drink and took a deep breath. "Rumours aside. Do you have anything else?"

Kennedy went through his notebook and seemed to hesitate over a number of items he had listed there, and then moved on. Finally, a thin smile touched his lips. "Resources." He paused for dramatic effect. "It appears the resources of the school are seriously lacking: a suitable classroom; residency arrangements for the teacher; learning materials. Unfortunately, without these, the school cannot remain open. So, from this moment, I have the authority to close this sham of education down."

McCray came and leaned over his shoulder. He spoke very slowly into his ear. "It is apparent to me Kennedy; you have no interest in representing the Board or supporting their educational goals. You have a personal agenda that is not yet clear to me. But something *is* clear: the only sham here is you. You didn't come to investigate; you came to shut us down. What you say is hogwash! I would challenge you to find a better-resourced school anywhere for the size of our community. We have an exceptional set-up, an exceptional teacher, and the student's results demonstrate that."

"I would have to disagree with you."

"Really? On what grounds?"

The deep boom of an explosion split the air. Kennedy's eyes turned to ice and the smirk across his face thinned out into a sneer. "The schoolhouse accidentally burnt down."

Lonnie ran into the room. "Master McCray, Master McCray! The schoolhouse – the schoolhouse," she said breathlessly, her accent getting the better of her. "Big bang! Much smoke!"

20.

Maggie stood before the smouldering ruins of the schoolhouse. Her vision spun in and out of focus, incomprehensible shock enveloping her. Everything in the classroom and her rooms had been demolished. Nothing remained excepting the rusty old windmill and the tank-stand, which teetered pathetically like a broken monument near a grave. She swayed unsteadily and Sammy tried to steer her away. She refused to go.

Duncan came and took her arm. "Maggie," he said through gritted teeth. "We have to go back."

"This is no review. We have been sabotaged from every side. Please tell me this is a nightmare. I want to wake up now."

"Poker, Maggie. Poker. I don't know what the agenda is."

"He *has* the best hand."

"That is what Poker is. Not letting them know. Can you do that?"

"I don't think so," she said with a shudder. "But I will try."

They walked into the Dining Room and McCray pulled out the chair for Maggie to sit. She sat pale and brittle in the chair. When she closed her eyes, the negative imprint of the flames engulfing her life consumed her vision. She gasped and opened her eyes wide. McCray sat down beside her and put his hand on her forearm, holding her steady.

Kennedy watched them and smirked. "Oh, look at this: fraternising with the schoolteacher. The Board dimly views romantic liaisons."

"You labour 'The Board' excessively Kennedy. We have had no support from the Board of General Education since the issue regarding the enrolments was raised. So, the reality is this: This is a private establishment – funded privately, and you have no authority to open or close anything because The Board has no vested interest in this school. Your actions amount to criminal destruction of property!"

"But there is no evidence we were involved in that tragedy. That was just very bad luck. There are, however, others who have a vested interest in this school."

"Do you care to elaborate? Henderson himself was supportive of this arrangement, and I cannot think how this situation could be of interest to anyone outside Henderson's Gap."

"There is a benefactor. Of course, it is their expressed wish to stay anonymous."

Duncan looked sceptical. "And I suppose this anonymous benefactor will magnanimously rebuild our school – just because of our unlucky misfortune? Come on Kennedy. You can't seriously think we believe you are part of the Board of General Education, nor that there is any benefactor."

"I showed you our letters of introduction."

McCray shrugged. "And who is impressed?"

Kennedy considered him and a smirk lingered under the glint in his eyes. It was his turn to shrug. "I am not here to impress. Actually, you are right on both accounts. I don't represent the Board of General Education and there is no private benefactor. Although I did feel our charade was inspiring. It was useful to get me here because I am being paid quite handsomely to deliver you a message."

McCray leaned back and pondered what he said. He felt Maggie stiffen. "See now, that interests me. Out here messages are infrequent, and generally anticipated."

Kennedy swung back in his chair and put his boots on the table. He laughed. "Oh, I hope so." He considered them both and smiled. Then he dropped his feet to the floor and stood up. "The message is this: the school closes; the schoolteacher leaves; and life goes back to normal."

"I suspect there is a qualifier included."

"Things go back to the way they were, or the tendency for buildings to spontaneously combust will continue. The tendency for cattle to go missing will continue. Hell, even kids may go missing."

McCray jumped to his feet coiled like a panther, ready to pounce. Maggie looked up; the pupils of her eyes wide. "The children? What do you mean?" Kennedy's assistant stood in the corner; the barrel of a gun emerged from his coat. Duncan eyed him warily, assessing his move.

Kennedy continued. "The situation is this. Some people are very distressed with the changes around here. My client has exerted their connections to apply a little pressure to help restore equilibrium in the matter."

Maggie went pale and gripped the arms of the chair. "*Connections?*" she gasped. "He wouldn't!" she whispered under her breath. Poker. Play poker! She spoke tersely. "You seem to think these 'connections' mean it is a done deal."

"Oh, you are right," he said smoothly with confidence. "I have every reason to believe you both will be anxious to comply with my client's wishes." He walked over to the sideboard and poured himself a drink, considered it and then passed the glass carelessly to McCray. "The thing is this: I hold the thing *you* hold most dear. And, should you feel there would be a change of heart in agreeing with these terms, that dear little son of yours, let's just say, he will go missing. So, I'll lay it out for you nice and clear. The school closes – the hard work on that has already been taken care of. The teacher goes back to wherever she comes from and does not return to Henderson's Gap. A deposit of £5000 will be made out to this account." He placed a sheet of paper before McCray. "And of course, no attempt will be made to trace our activity. You see. Life has so many choices."

Kennedy came over to stand behind Maggie and pulled a handgun from his inside pocket. He leant down and whispered in her ear. "You embrace this opportunity and his son will be fine. If... if you so much as *blink* in the wrong direction, he will *not* be fine." He ran the barrel of his handgun over her shoulder. Maggie shuddered in horror. He stared at Duncan directly. "As for the schoolteacher, such a pretty thing. If *you* decide not to go along with this, I guarantee you, her face will not please so well; her eyes will not see as well; her tongue will not speak as well. All teacher assets. Hypothetically speaking of course."

McCray picked up the glass and took a sip and hurled it at Kennedy's head across the room. He calmly ducked as it hit the wall, crystal splintering across the room in a thousand pieces. Maggie dived under the table.

Kennedy returned to the sideboard and calmly took another glass. "Yeah, I know, kidnapping and extortion – such ugly words. But really, what choice do I have? I need you to choose wisely." He stared at his glass as he lightly swirled it. He focused on the whirlpool in the amber liquid as his offsider pulled Maggie out from under the table holding her firmly. Kennedy continued. "Of course, McCray, there would be a level of incompleteness to this scenario for you to remain untouched. So, we have a guarantee for you too. Your name becomes a disgrace, years in the penitentiary for duffing. With the right combination of offences, there will eventually be a hanging. Hypothetically speaking of course." All in all, he seemed quite satisfied he had summed up the situation acceptably.

"So, if I leave… if I *just* leave… this all goes away?" Maggie's whisper was hoarse with bewilderment.

"So succinct, Miss Wick. I can see why you are a very good teacher. Don't forget the five thousand pounds. Which sounds such a meagre price for the things we value."

☙•❧

Duncan and Maggie's hands were bound tightly, and they were pushed outside into the glaring sunlight. Kennedy's men stayed close, the barrels of their guns poking under their ribs, kept them quiet. Thelma held Alex protectively behind her on the verandah, his little face white with fear.

Kennedy stood on the steps and watched with a presiding smirk. As they were led past, Kennedy announced with a sneer, "I'm going to give you some time to consider the things we discussed. You have until sundown to give your commitment to the terms we discussed. The boy stays with me until we get the money."

There were horses tethered near the gate. They mounted up and sat dazed in the saddles with their hands bound. Then the horses were led out. What Duncan found beyond explanation was that Kennedy would show his hand. The man had such impenetrable assurance. It was like he had taken out every card and savoured his brilliance by laying them on the table. Duncan had to assume such indomitable confidence meant that he also had an ace or two hidden up his sleeve.

One of Kennedy's underlings rode Maestro in a bold display of arrogance. Following a trail through the scrub, they paused the horses for a moment, and then, through the trees they saw Blondie appear, his black broad face sober with shame. "We go'n this way," he said pointing, not looking at either of them. And he followed the track to the right, which led further up into the hills towards a rocky outcrop.

Maggie stared ahead. Blondie was Judas? She had argued his loyalty with Duncan, but it was hard to dispute his tall frame scooting through the bush, light on his bare feet, escorting them into the deep scrub. She watched the shadows dancing off his bare, ceremonially scarred back, and his spears bobbing in time with his long gait as he led them away from the homestead.

Duncan was a soldier, yet the rage in his mind was building like the pressure gauge on a steam engine. He closed his eyes and evened his breathing. Think.

He had to think strategically. They had Alex. They had Maggie. They were being taken away, isolated and hidden; cut off from those he might collaborate with. He couldn't physically bravado his way out of this. He had to fight with his mind: strategy, chess.

Maggie glanced over at Duncan riding beside her. His eyes were focused, scanning for information, vying for his next best move. She knew that look. And it infused her with the hope that perhaps the situation was not as overwhelming as it seemed. But when their captors rode up beside her, and their coats fell open and she saw more guns strapped professionally to their side, she had to reconsider the odds. They might have presented as incompetent bookkeepers, but it was clear these men possessed skills not initially disclosed. They had no scruples about blowing apart her life and incinerating the schoolhouse to the ground. Even if Duncan could orchestrate their escape, the danger that entrapped Alex was undeniably tight.

21.

They sat against the side of a cave, ropes digging raw lines into their wrists. Duncan had the distinct privilege of understanding their grim position. He reviewed in his mind what he knew. He knew Kennedy wasn't the mind behind the game – it was a safe bet he was the hired help, but hired by who? His involvement was probably nothing more than the aspiration to develop a darker reputation on the market as an excellent option. Mercenaries with a reputation could ask for more. He knew Maggie was the key to unravelling this bizarre turn of events, but he didn't know how. It hardly seemed enough. The only small mercy was that Alex had been allowed to stay with Thelma. At least he had a familiar friend through this trauma.

He had noted how Maggie had easily tasted the flavour of Hastings in this. What had he learnt about Leon Hastings that night at dinner? He was arrogant, smooth and not prone to be reasonable. If he wanted something it was likely he would go after it without a twinge of conscience. Was this an ostentatious play to claim Maggie back? Duncan's contempt for the man did not underestimate the danger he saw behind the facade of suave talk and engaging stories. Bland, he may be, but benign? Oh no, Duncan was confident he had got that wrong. He was not 'benign'.

There were other people disenchanted with the changes around Henderson's Gap. Lonnie didn't do so well with change. He had no doubt Sammy's claims were accurate: if Lonnie wanted to, she could take him out. But not Maggie. She would never sabotage the passion of her daughter like that.

Casey was the not only parent who had objected outright about having "natives" in the classroom, but they had taken the line of least resistance and conceded to allow the school to operate as it was... for now. Mostly McCray attributed this unusual racial tolerance to the exceptional opportunity of having a local school and the need for enrolment numbers. And he couldn't dismiss the high opinion the community held for Jones. The man was well-liked. Yet as numbers on the school roll increased, he would not be surprised if these parents demanded that the education of their children be different to what the school at Henderson's Gap offered. The escalating interest in the Removal Policy seemed to indicate locals still held to the thinking that segregation worked best. But McCray had to admit the elaborate subterfuge and dramatic connections were not Casey's style. He was not the sharpest tool in the box. Besides, he couldn't imagine where he would get the type of money required to engage the services of someone like Kennedy.

He looked over at Blondie. He was a master on a stock horse and worked with cattle just as intuitively. A natural athlete, a skilled hunter, the best tracker Duncan had ever witnessed, and fearless. In a different place and different era, Generals would have enlisted him to lead battle charges against enemy barbarian tribes. Here he was the barbarian. Blondie stood still as stone, a silent silhouette standing against the wall of the cave, his rough foot resting relaxed on his knee like a one-legged stork. He seemed almost asleep, yet suspiciously positioned with a view of the track leading to the mouth of the cave, and still maintained a visual where both he and Maggie were held prisoner. So, he had been right: Blondie had gone renegade. He was the reason the stock duffing had been unexplainably untraceable after all. Kennedy unapologetically had turned him.

Duncan closed his eyes. He went over it all again, and again. Perhaps he had missed something. Anything? The pieces were positioned. He had no move. "Checkmate," he muttered quietly.

Maggie looked at him. "No!" she whispered. "I will not concede. I will not go out without a fight. And I will not give up until the last move is played."

"This is not a board-game where I can sweep the pieces into a heap. The play is set."

"There has to be something."

"If there is – I don't see it. There is no way. I lose."

"Not just you. Us. We all lose."

He looked at the desperate plea in her eyes. "I'm sorry Maggie. If it were my life they valued, the next move would be clear, but they know there is no bargaining a life one would willingly give. But I can't sacrifice either you or Alex. Please forgive me. I can't play it that way."

"I know... I know..." Tears rolled down her face. "I just don't think I can either. How will I ever...?" A peewee called out over the rocky landscape and Maggie's heart broke as she listened to the duet song calling back and forwards, sharp and clear. "Did you know... you made my heart hear the duet of a peewee? They always sing in pairs, never alone. Our song is over before it is sung." It called again to its mate; flaunting its companionship in is raucous rhythm. "Oh, why won't it give up?"

Duncan felt the tension in his shoulders knot just a little tighter. His Queen, after all this time, he had found his White Queen. He sat as the implications washed over him, and he still struggled to know his next move.

৯•৩

As morning dawned Duncan took a deep breath and steadied his pulse. His sleep had been light, like other mornings as he readied for battle. He closed his eyes, clearing his mind. Kennedy had given them to sundown, yet they had not come demanding their answer. That meant something had changed. Hope soared, heightening his senses. His breathing became even. He sat for a moment, absorbing the feel of the morning. And he looked down at Maggie dozing in the dust beside him, leaning on his shoulder.

Their guards were restless. They obviously had not slept. Blondie, on the other hand, still stood silently on guard duty at the mouth of the cave. One started flicking pebbles at a rock, in a fidgety sort of way. The other referred to his fob-watch, again and again, tucking it back into his vest pocket with an agitated twist to unkink the chain. After a while, the rock-flicking underling stood up and offered a crass explanation for his need to go back into the dark of the cave. Blondie's body did not move but McCray watched his eyes follow him. The fob-watch minion went over to Blondie, and waved his clock in his dark face, muttering fiercely.

Blondie tolerated the verbal barrage for a bit, then he put his leg down and stood up straight. He spoke slowly. "But Misser, you don't understand. I only used to moving targets, like wallaby. You cut him loose: I get him straight down the middle like big-man kangaroo."

Duncan didn't move, but his senses came on full alert, and he kept his eyes half closed, trying to give the appearance he was still asleep.

He swore and shook his head. He flicked open his fob-watch again. "You can't be serious. I've never heard of that before."

Blondie shrugged and put his foot back on his knee nonplussed. "Ever been hunting with a black-fella? Ever seen a 'roo sit still while someone's gunna eat him?"

"Well, you try now. The boss was very clear: time is up. We have no margin. We have to go to Plan B. Then your job is done. You'll still get paid. Then you can go."

"No worries Boss, but like I said: he has to run. See. Me show ya." Blondie came towards them with his spears. He looked serious; his mouth grim. He spat on the ground and made paint out of the dust, which he smeared across his chest. He started to dance in short clipped steps kicking up the dust, chanting in a low voice.

Maggie opened her eyes and sat up straight staring at him mortified, her face went pale. Her eyes narrowed intently like watching a snake. Suddenly she understood exactly what was going down. She turned to Duncan who sat motionless, not even awake yet, and then she twisted away, was sick and passed out. She toppled sideways, her face in the dust.

Blondie picked up the pace of his dance. He hurled his spear. It hit the wall beside McCray's head, and with a loud thud, it landed beside him. With a double-quick fluid motion, he pulled a knife from his trousers and with a twang it embedded in the ground near Duncan's tied hands. Suddenly he stopped. He shrugged with embarrassment. He pointed. "See. Big shame for hunter. But I hit him moving," he said hopefully. "I gunna try again. I will..." He bent down and spat again and made more paint.

"No, no... don't bother. I get the point. Cut him loose then."

"Well, you might want to do that, Boss. Don't want him getting away."

"What? I thought you said you can get him on the run!"

"Well sure. But if I have to untie him, and then skewer him..." he shrugged. "So just to be sure Plan B doesn't go haywire, you cut him loose and I'll be ready when he runs." He restarted his chant and dance.

The guard impatiently cut the ropes on McCray's ankles and stood him to his feet. "Now run you..." He never finished his sentence. He gasped and clutched the spear protruding from his shoulder. "Oops... missed again," Blondie said shyly, as he quickly tackled and tied him like a steer bolting for the fray. He spun around but Duncan had already loosed his hands with the knife, and threw it, just as the other fellow emerged buttoning his trousers. He grabbed at his thigh, squealing like a pig. They gagged and tied him beside the other. There was a pause.

"Capt'n…" Blondie said in the silence, acknowledging him with a nod.

"Blondie," said McCray and he shook his hand fervently, as equals. They pulled the writhing bodies over against the opposite wall of the cave, into the dark shadows, out of sight. Duncan lifted Maggie out of the dust and brushed the hair from her face. "Is there water?"

Blondie handed him a flask apologetically. "She didn't need to see this. Good thing she passed out Capt'n; saved me having to explain myself."

Duncan loosened the buttons at her collar and wiped her face with a damp kerchief. She moaned slightly. "She wasn't sure which camp you were in," he said.

Blondie smiled. "The way she hit the dust Capt'n, I reckon she thought there was no doubt."

"Well, your bad aim was too precise. I've seen you split a fly on a canvas."

"White-fellas don't have a clue. Make stuff up and they swallow it whole."

Duncan acknowledged with a nod that somehow, he had been excluded from that blanket brainless white population. He wiped Maggie's face again.

Blondie seemed to have found his voice. "They must think I'm a half-wit: *do job, get paid, go home?* Sure, and they throw in flour and sugar for the missus.

Capt'n, this ain't over. They've been working up to it too long."

Duncan grimaced and went to say something, but as Maggie's lids fluttered open, he looked gently into her eyes. "There you are. Welcome back."

Blondie looked agitated. "Capt'n! I'm reckoning they'll be heading on after ya boy. Gotta go!" Blondie gathered his weapons.

"Alex?"

Blondie nodded.

"Do you know where they were taking him?"

"Jones said he'd take him to the camp if he could. He figured that'd be the last place they'd go looking for him, and best to keep him safe out of the way."

McCray looked at him and swore. "Alex could be at the camp? As in your camp? With the Elders?" He swore again. "They'll use it as an excuse to take the whole place apart. We have to get there – be ready for them." Duncan steadied Maggie's arm as she tried to protest. "Who knows about this cave?"

Blondie shook his head. "Just the men and the Elders."

"Jones?"

"Of course."

Duncan propped Maggie up against the wall of the cave. "Maggie, listen: you can't go back to the Homestead. Stay here, this place is safe. I'm going with Blondie to the camp. They've declared war." He picked over their coats, removing their handguns and rifles. He also found another knife. He handed some pieces to Blondie. "Maggie, I'll leave you one of the horses. If this all goes wrong, just leave. Get as far away as possible. Promise me!" The intensity of his voice shocked her senses. She nodded mutely. "And take this…" He checked a small handgun and passed it to her. "You might need it," he said to Maggie as he left his flask beside her and mounted Maestro, following Blondie to war.

22.

Maggie sat in the silence. The morning sun already glared angrily at the mouth of the cave. She felt dazed and exhausted. She didn't fully comprehend what had happened, but her confidence was bolstered knowing Duncan was no longer bound. He was able to make his moves freely and unfettered. And now he would make sure Alex was safe. Nothing else mattered. For one who had sat motionless, for an indeterminable amount of time, it felt like she had rowed multiple races back to back. Her body ached. It reminded her of how she felt as a kid after branding steers with Jones. Every muscle hurt. She stretched and moved around a little, sluggish and exhausted. Then she crumpled her shawl into a cushion and lay down again and went to sleep.

As Maggie slept, she heard the peewee call. Again, and again, it echoed harshly in her sleep. She wanted so much to believe in that invitation, that there would be a duet like this she could sing. She wanted to believe that this music would be a persistent, common, everyday song; one to sing any time of day; safe and ordinary. She struggled to the surface of her sleep, groggy and disorientated. She felt the dust between her fingers, intrigued by the texture of it.

Then Maggie felt the shadows move and her senses became alert, focused and wary. Her muscles tensed as she remembered the handgun. She crept her hand under her shawl. Her fingers wrapped around the handle, finding the trigger. It felt strangely unfamiliar. It was a long time since she was twelve and held a rifle under the watchful eye of Jones.

A quiet voice behind her whispered, "Miss Maggie... got a message... and some tucker."

She sighed with relief. "Tom?"

"Yeah... it's me. Please, you can take your hand away now."

"Oh." She looked around. "Are you alone?"

"Yeah. Dad sent me."

She moved her hand from under her shawl and sat up. Everything was reddish-brown from the dirt. She tried to tidy her hair and brushed her sleeves down. "You have a message?"

"Yeah. Alex is safe. He's okay. Dad got him away."

"He's safe," she echoed, and her shoulders relaxed. Maggie closed her eyes, visibly relieved, thanking God for his protection. She looked at the pendant fob watch on her neck-chain. It was mid-morning: half ten. "What a relief! Duncan got there in time."

"The Capt'n? I never saw him."

"But you said they got away?"

"Away from the homestead and those men. Alex is at the camp. He'll be okay there. They're my cousins," he added in case she didn't fully understand.

"Oh." She hadn't eaten since yesterday. "You said you had food?"

Tom nodded seriously. "Misses Lonnie said it give you energy."

"It *will* give you energy," she corrected instinctively.

"Actually, Misses Lonnie did say..." Tom smiled cheekily. "Miss Maggie not as beat up as she looks. She's okay." He handed her some sandwiches made with Lonnie's famous jam.

She divided them in half and offered the other portion to Tom. "So, Lonnie is okay?" she said as she took a bite. The sandwiches hadn't travelled well. Still, Lonnie would always find a way to look after her own. Tom nodded and hunkered down beside her. Maggie took a drink from the flask and handed it to Tom. He drank and handed it back. She felt herself revive as she slowly ate. She didn't feel that hungry. She made sure Tom ate something too. She took another drink and screwed on the lid.

"Feeling better? How did you get here? Did you ride?"

He nodded. "I shadowed. Miss Maggie, there are men all over the place. They got people from town."

"Keren, Andy and the others... where are they?"

"Just shadowing, but not near the camp. Dad wanted them away. Just in case they were out for a Taking. Misses Lonnie gave me some food to take to them too."

"... and Sammy... is he okay?"

He hesitated. "Sammy... they beat him up some. He's tough though."

Maggie sat still. She felt numb. Was this all really happening? Somehow life had suddenly turned dangerous. Something niggled in her mind. Something important. Something Duncan had said...

"So, you didn't see Blondie either?"

"Na. Dad's had me running all over the place – between Lonnie and the others. Plus, when you're shadowing... sometimes you have to go around and it takes longer. Saw tracks though, but I dunno whose horse. Blondie can tell which horse it is. Mostly anyway."

"Blondie can tell which horse it is by the tracks it makes?"

Tom nodded. "Mostly," he repeated. To him, it was as unremarkable as Miss Maggie fluently reading a difficult book out loud to the class. He couldn't do that either... yet.

This thing, this niggly thing, plagued her. Did she hear something? She looked towards the recess of the blackness. Muffled moans of ghosts seemed to echo around the cave. She shivered and stood up; wobbling slightly as her stiff legs cramped. She edged back into the dim corners of the cave. Her eyes, adjusted... making out they were... something... she wasn't sure. "Tom go check that no one is coming." As he went to the mouth of the cave, Maggie edged close and blinked as she identified bulges... coats... and then it struck her – Kennedy's men, their eyes, fiery and wild. A bloodied ooze seeped through their rudimentary, unsympathetic bandages.

She loosened the gags and offered a drink. A volley of curses and threats gushed out like vomit. One spat a bloodied mess over the front of her dress. She hurriedly readjusted to gags to protect Tom's ears. She turned away quickly, acid gagging in her throat. Staying here was no longer an option. Then it dawned on her what he had said: the camp. The men were on the way there. Not for peace, but for war. Alex was there. Duncan had said that they *had* declared war. Even if they would never 'take' a white child, Alex was right in the middle of a battle-zone. She had to get to him. Then they could go into the bush with the others and stay in the shadows until everything was over. If she needed to go far away, just as Duncan said, Alex would be with her. Duncan's son...

It is one thing to have an intention; it is another to bring it to pass. Maggie went to heave the saddle off the ground, but Tom shook his head slowly. "You can't shadow... on a horse... Miss Maggie... they too big. Dad made me promise… only to shadow." His speech was slurring.

"We have to walk?" Her voice sounded weirdly petulant to Maggie's ears. As she turned around a cloud of cotton wool hit her. Her mind felt so fuzzy. She needed the horse in case of… She blinked her eyes hard and shook her head, forcing herself to focus. She struggled to know what needed to be done. She leaned against the wall of the cave, supporting her legs as they wavered weakly underneath her. She looked over at Tom sitting on the ground staring vacantly at the sky. She closed her eyes for a moment and then shook herself awake. "Tom…" He didn't move. She struggled over to him. She shook him by the shoulder. "Tom…"

He stared at her vacantly. "Tom… come back inside. I think we are going to have to rest awhile. Lonnie's energy lunch is not working…" She knew perfectly well it was working just as Lonnie intended. She wanted to keep Maggie away, silenced by slumber. They huddled back in the shadows of the cave and had no choice but to surrender to sleep.

❧•❧

When Maggie came to, the shadows were lengthening. She looked at her fob watch and concentrated on the position of the hands. Everything was fuzzy. Alex? She tried to remember and with a nauseous rush, it came. She leant over and was sick. Alex. She had no idea how long it was since Duncan left. But she knew she had to get to Alex.

She checked Tom and he was breathing regularly. She made her way to the horse, struggling to lift the saddle, fumbling the girth and stirrup straps. She shook Tom's awake. She didn't have a clue about how to get to the camp by herself. "Tom!" she said urgently. "Tom. It is time to go. We must go to the camp..."

Tom opened his eyes and grinned stupidly. "Miss Maggie. I did my homework." He closed his eyes and started snoring again.

"Tom! Wake up. We have to go… to help your Dad. Yes, he needs us now. It is our turn..." She felt it was a little unfair playing on his loyalty like that, but *she* needed help. "Tom, get up now… time to go." She trickled some water from the canteen over his closed eyes and he spluttered as it ran into his mouth. And rolled over snoring. With hazy inspiration, she picked up their unfinished lunch beside the canteen, and she went back to the prisoners. She loosened their gags and offered them a drink and a sandwich. She sat and waited as they ate, and slowly their eyes glazed over. She left the canteen with them and tried not to think about how they could possibly use it while still bound… when their sedation began to wear off.

She shook Tom's shoulder again.

He stirred. "Shadow... is it time to shadow now?" he muttered.

"Yes. I've saddled the horse. We are ready to leave."

"Can't shadow on a horse Miss Maggie..." he insisted sleepily.

She felt groggy. Walking hardly seemed plausible. "I know... but we need to take him to the creek for a drink. We can't leave him here. We'll stop before we get too close to the camp and then go the rest of the way on foot. Would that work?"

"Okay," he reluctantly conceded, even though Maggie could tell it didn't meet his expectations of a purist shadower. Not at all.

For some reason, she felt emotion rise in her throat. This boy was an exceptional young man, and she was privileged to have him with her as her guide. "Thank you, Tom," she said softly. It seemed so inadequate. "Thank you..."

He heard the catch in her voice and turned around to look at her. "You welcome Miss Maggie. You family now."

Her eyes smiled as she realised the compliment was generous. "I'm glad – you are too, my Shadow-boy."

She climbed into the saddle, hoisted Tom up in front of her and turned towards the camp. It was like walking through a cloud. Hazy and grey; the world seemed out of focus. Every so often they would stop, and Tom would look around confused. Then, as if recalibrating, they would start on again. The hairs on Maggie's arms began to rise the further they went. A foreboding crept over them and settled like a net, strangling. She could feel Tom's body stiffen.

She stopped the horse. "Can we can walk from here?" She didn't want to go any further, she really didn't. How would she ever find them? What if...? Her mind screamed at the terror that surrounded her. She dismounted hoping that the feel of the earth under her feet would somehow swallow her and silence the fear. She looked at the boy beside her, struggling with a premonition that was floating like evil ghosts. "Tom?"

"Miss Maggie..." his eyes filled with tears, anxiety rising.

"What would your Dad do now?"

Tom blinked, through the fog. He knew what his Dad would do. "He'd pray; that the evil would go and that peace would come... and then for courage to do what needed to be done."

"We need that too."

Tom nodded and folded his hands. "Jesus, Big Boss of Heaven and Earth. In your name, we tell fear to go because your love chucks fear out and we ask peace to come and be at home in us instead. We pray your Spirit get us courage to do what needs to be done... and wisdom. Dad prays for wisdom a lot. He says it doesn't mean you're stupid, it's just common sense to take advice… especially God's advice 'cause he knows everything there is to know. In Jesus' name. Amen."

"Amen."

"You gotta pray now Miss Maggie… and agree. Mum does that."

"Lord Jesus… I agree with Tom. For peace, wisdom and courage. Amen."

"Now we just gotta step out and do the next thing. That's what Dad says."

"The next thing is…"

"… shadow to the camp."

Maggie's mind raced. She dreaded finding out what had gone down. She had the most appalling sense of tragedy fill her senses and she wondered if she should leave now, go far away, and not face whatever catastrophe lay around the corner. She needed to find something to divert Tom away. She suddenly understood why Jones had his son running errands all over the countryside, taking bread and messages from one end of the station to another. And why Lonnie tried to keep them immobilised. But she could not ignore what she knew: as awful, as painful, as unsafe and horrific as it might be. She had to.

She stopped. "Tom?" She looked at his eyes, clouded with this aura of undefined pain. She couldn't think of any diversion that would not seem contrived.

Tom grimaced and shrugged. "Yeah, I know. We need to go back to the homestead and find Alex's little bear, the one with the chewed ear. Dad said he might need it."

She raised her eyebrows. Jones had anticipated a number of worthy missions for his son. "Something familiar and comforting might help him," she agreed.

Tom shrugged with grown-up responsibility weighing on his shoulders. Each assignment was important. "He's just a kid. It might..."

"And to have that bear with us when we meet him would be better than fetching it later, don't you think?"

Tom considered this and gravely nodded his head. "Yep. He won't have to feel sad then," he said simply. Then he paused seriously. "Miss Maggie, I mean no disrespect, but it would be quicker for me to go by myself."

She deliberately appeared to take his remark to heart. "But I thought I was learning to shadow well." Tom looked embarrassed and stared at his bare feet, so Maggie lightly tugged his sleeve with a grin. "I know... just not *that* well. Can you do it without being seen?" He rolled his eyes at the obvious, so she didn't hesitate any longer. "I think you are right – it might be better for you to do this by yourself. And Tom, thank you."

He disappeared into the shadows, and Maggie allowed herself an internal sigh. She could not have anticipated that at all and she praised Jones for his wisdom. Now. To the camp.

Maggie heard before she saw. It was the awful sound of madness and fear. It pervaded the trees, and the soil, and the settling evening dew. She held herself, desperately restraining every nerve-fibre, allowing it to draw her closer and closer instead of running in panic. She stood paralysed in the brush of clustered tea-trees on the fringe of the camp clearing, surveying the war-scape before her. Bodies lay writhing; women were moaning and wailing, racked with anguish over a loved one who lay bleeding. And in the centre of it all, Duncan stood, presiding over the horror seething around him.

Revulsion filled her. Duncan courted this agony. He pursued this horror and he was unmoved by the trauma of those injured and destroyed in the process. With the common ease of a conductor on a train, he moved amongst the horror and snapped out instructions. She recognised no one until she saw him talk with Blondie, and tie a bandana to a bloodied wound on his upper arm.

She moved forward, slowly like the horrible ghosts hovering around her, floating in and about the blood-stained dirt. She turned around, unable to decide what to do. She stepped on someone's arm and gasped in horror. They did not move.

Duncan saw her then, his eyes becoming unreadable. He strode to her side and held her. "Maggie? You should not be here."

She pulled away. "So, I would not see you in this? What vile evil!"

He read her contempt. "The evil was well on its way before we arrived. But since you are here, you will help." His tone was firm, unsympathetic, cold, authoritative.

"Ride to the homestead. Help Lonnie prepare places, as many as you can: in the dining room, verandah, anywhere: to tend the wounded. Tear sheets into bandages. We will take them there. Get Sammy to bring back all the horses, plus hessian and ropes. Some of these people can't walk or ride. We'll need stretchers." As he spoke, he led her to where some wild-eyed horses were tethered. When he hoisted her up onto Maestro, emotion choked in her throat. At this moment she would trade anything not to ride his stallion. Duncan handed her the reigns. "Don't spare him; time will save lives here."

Maestro stamped the ground, and she turned his head towards home. He jumped forward into a gallop, sinew and power straining forward, the smell of blood and panic pressing him urgently on. She leant forward, her shoulders moulding over his neck. The horse thundered towards home, a gash in his flank ripping open with fresh blood, as he jumped ditches and logs in an intuitive dash of mercy. The setting sun spilt red smears across the horizon, staining the earth, soaking up the screams and the panic, the pain and the horror.

23.

Maggie leapt from the saddle and went straight through the kitchen calling out as she bounded up the stairs. And she worked furiously with Lonnie to transform Henderson's Gap homestead into a war-hospital. As they started to arrive, she ran outside and helped them limp inside. Wailing crowded the airspace alongside moans.

She fumbled with bandages and hurried on to the next need. She urgently padded up another wound. She came to where Lonnie knelt holding a cup of sedative to crusted lips and signalled for another to come and sit, respectfully offering dignity as they faded out of this life. The Captain went ahead with a suturing kit rolled in a leather bundle. It was rudimentary at best. Lonnie floated among the mats giving advice in Mandarin when she was feeling too strained to translate her thinking. It never occurred to her that advice no one could understand would be no advice at all.

Duncan came and stood beside Maggie on the verandah. He was exhausted, but he knew battle lines, and the lines within himself. It would be days yet before he would stop, and he also knew that this storm he had created would be on its way back to meet him. They may have retreated. But they would return with reinforcements. "Maggie. I haven't seen Alex. Do you know? Have you heard anything?"

Maggie gasped. The realisation that from the moment she stood in the tea-tree brush beside the camp-clearing her mind had been consumed with pain. Little Alex, the very reason for her foray into the chaos, somehow had been lost. The catch in her throat constricted. "I... I don't know. I went there... to get him away. I'm so sorry Duncan. I went there for Alex."

"I can't find Thelma; thought maybe she might know. At the camp, I asked Jones' oldest girl to take him, since he knew her from school. They went with some of the women who had kids. They were splitting up. I haven't seen any of them."

"Oh Duncan, do you think they are still out there? He'll be terrified." She trembled with the thought. "Please take me with you. Tom came back to get his bear. He didn't want him to be frightened."

"I'm not sure we can do anything until it gets light, but I'll ask Blondie. Get the bear and Tom. If Blondie thinks there's a possibility of finding him, I want you there." What he wanted was her away from this seething mass of grief.

Blondie looked at the darkened night sky. It seemed that even the stars had cloaked themselves in grief. "Darkest night on the calendar. We could get close. But we could also walk two feet away and miss them. They know not to show themselves when they're hidin' in the shadows."

They set out, the only sound was the spluttering of the torches that they held high, and the tramp of their feet. The camp was silent with death. One small campfire and three tired elders sat vigil to keep dingos at bay. One played a didgeridoo, mournful rhythms pulsating out into the dark. There was no end to the depths of horror that echoed in their dark eyes. Bodies were covered in hessian waiting for their ceremonies.

Blondie sat down in silence by the fire. Maggie felt agitated. Surely, they must know something. After a long-extended pause, Blondie spoke quietly; and each one sadly shook their head. The women who left with the children had not come back. They had not heard them. With respect and with silence, Blondie stood and backed away.

Tom knew where he had delivered their last food parcel and led the way there. Blondie studied the area in the torchlight. A smoky yellow glow danced a weird corroboree on the trunks of the trees. Maggie slumped down and pressed her palms against her eye-sockets hoping it might ease the pressure she felt there. Would the nightmare ever end? She was being sucked further down this swirling mire of horror and it was getting more ghastly by the moment. And then, as if insult overlaid torment, the piping of a peewee split the night air. She groaned. How much more?

Duncan's eyes became alert. "Peewee..." he said, and leant over Maggie and whispered cryptically, "The peewee sings in the shadows. Watch for the shadows."

Her gut flipped. She dropped her hands and looked about. Could there be any deeper shadows than those of an outback night? Blondie spoke quietly to Tom, and then to her amazement, she saw Tom pull something from his pocket and raise it to his mouth, and clearly pipe the call of a peewee chime. The notes struck sharp and clear. Tom was singing peewee. And just like his feathered counterparts, there responded a call, faint, but definite, the call of family, a duet. Blondie signalled to him to keep chiming as his dark frame disappeared into the night shadows.

Maggie listened mesmerised. Tom called back, waiting for the syncopated response to echo their position. The sound was so true. How many times had she heard this song, or had it been Tom and his sisters, mimicking? Again, he called. Faintly they heard a response.

Then there was the deep silence of a bush night in mourning. Duncan signalled to Tom to call again. He did, but it sounded harsh and off-note. Again... and this time the notes faltered. Tears welled up. Maggie came and put her hand on his shoulder. "It's okay Tom. Let's wait for a moment. You play the peewee's song?"

He shrugged. "It's our call, our secret. Blondie said it's still secret, 'cause we're family here. Those not family – they still don't know."

Maggie smiled. "Blondie is not only the world's best tracker; he is smart too."

"Ma'am, me hearing that," said Blondie as he emerged from among the trees and shrubs. She nodded slightly in the torchlight, covered by her exclaims of relief when she saw the women with him, one carried Alex sleeping in her arms, his little shirt covered in blood. A trail of kids following; Priscilla, Jemima and the older girls giving the little ones piggybacks. The woman went to the Captain and handed him his son. Duncan took him with relief, holding him tight.

৵•৶

Blondie sat still and silent against the rail of the verandah. He resisted being inside; it was too enclosed. He looked down the rail where lanterns shone pale in the night. Mat beside mat held his wounded, traumatised family, stoically, quietly moaning their grief. Maggie came and stood beside him. "Lonnie wants to look at your arm if you are able..." She looked at his angry, grief-stricken eyes. "She is good at what she does. Her medicine... it may help."

Blondie looked down at her, glazed. "Do ya know what I don't get?"

Maggie could only guess at a fraction of it. "How hate can wreak so much havoc? I don't get that."

"I don't get why a little white Gin was sent to us. Who would have thought that God would do that?"

"Lonnie?"

"You."

"Me? Why would you think that? Kennedy said if I went away... it would stop. I should have not hesitated. I should not have tried to fight it. If I had just gone away..."

"Jones... he ain't got long on this land. Soon his story will be silent. But you gotta know. Jones came here a green-horn. But he stubborn... he be part of this here. He said, "I can't understand your boots Blondie, I gotta walk in them... I wanta to do your work." He worked harder than ten other hands put together. No wonder Boss put him in charge. But even when Henderson make him head-stockman, he never get too good for the ordinary fellas. Jones says to me, "I got more boots to travel in..." He hung around like a fly on a hot sticky day. Couldn't get rid of him. He learnt the ways. He initiated: he my brother." He paused and looked out over the verandah. "Olivia my sister but not..." Blondie's voice became very quiet. "My mother was raped when she just a new wife..." He spat his distaste and anger. "That's Liv's curse. I never understand how one so beautiful come from such ugly. Jones was absolutely smitten with her. Liv told me she had found her place... that it was God's plan for her. Jones absolutely refused to shack up. He said he figured that if God meant for them fellow's to be together, there had to be a way to do it... in real life, proper like. My aunt spoke for him to the elders ... so they could marry." His focus seemed to fade, but then he suddenly resumed his musings. "Jones and the Capt'n – they got along... but something changed when you got here. I'm not sure Capt'n would have done what he did today, even six months ago... without you. You've got to know; Jones didn't agree about the cattle. But he never said nothing... he just went away to his spot and prayed."

"Cattle?"

"Those goons, them wanted to pin it on the Capt'n; they figured I'd do anything for my mob. Right too. I was bailed up. But I found a way... just like Jones said. Took 'em out the back, just ten or fifteen head at a time. They've lost a bit of condition, but safe enough. I haven't told the Capt'n where they are yet. Waiting for the dust to settle..."

He paused a moment, thoughtfully. "They'll run him through the wringer for this. *He* could end up being Taken as well. If you've got any praying left in you Maggie, now is the time to be praying for the Capt'n. He has done an unforgivable thing. He fought white fellas in defence of blackfellas. He saved my mob. Without him, we would be just another mob that no longer has a place or a memory. But we're still here. Torn up, but not destroyed. It's not just Taking our kids that plagues our people. It's Taking everything: our land, our lives."

Blondie left to see those he loved dearest; his own wounds forgotten. Duncan called Maggie over. He pulled back Jones' collar, revealing an old shirt that was stuffed in to pad up a wound on his shoulder. It had soaked through the dirty folds and had done nothing to stem the bleeding. Beside him lay Olivia, silent and cold, blood from her belly drenching her dress and the mat on which she lay. Duncan took off his coat and covered her.

Jones laid back against the wall, his face contorted as he propped himself up. Jones reached out his blood-soaked arm and rested his hand on his son's chest. "Tom, boy," he whispered, "God has good plans for you son. He promised. He will finish the things He started. In here... protect it in here. You have to forgive. Remind your brothers... sisters... your mother wants that. And we'll see you later... okay? This is... not the end."

Maggie lent down and pressed another pad against the wound. Tears soaked her lashes. "Jones... hold on!" she whispered. "Lonnie is skilled... we can fix this."

He barely shook his head. "God knows... I'm willing now, but later... I'm not sure. Knowing what they did... to Liv, and our baby... our family... perhaps this is best."

"Jones..."

His voice was faint. "Maggie. God brought you back. Take care of my girls... They are Princesses... in The Kingdom. Neutral ground... not many get that... but you do. Help Capt'n... with my boys... mind your shoes... God will guide..." He paused, his eyes brimming with overwhelming grief. "God forgive 'em... they haven't a clue."

Tom knelt before his Dad, silent and grim, violence stealing years before his very eyes. The light in his father's eyes flickered and went out, and his stare became vacant. Duncan reached down and closed his lids. And pulled the brim of his stockman's hat down over his face.

Duncan knelt down and rested his hand on Tom's shoulder. "Son, I'm so sorry..." and he held him as he bawled heartbroken into his shoulder.

Maggie stayed and looked out over where the school-house had stood just a few days ago, and wondered how the world could collapse so completely into a vortex of darkness in such a short time. She tried not to scream. She took a deep breath, and another... and another. If only she could keep breathing.

౿•ౚ

24.

"Your Honour, I will call the next witness: Miss Thelma Thane."

Maggie sat quietly, her face serenely pale. Yet inside she felt like a volcano ready to explode, spewing lava and ash all over the courtroom. Blondie's words ran around and around in her mind: *"If there be any praying left in you..."* She could not remember a time when there had been such violence and fervour in her prayers. Duncan sat in the trial dock. Subdued and masked, his military training rising to the severity of the situation. Four white men had died: Kennedy, two of his men, and Jones. Those in the cave survived their wounds. Nine full-blood aboriginals died, three of those children; and then Olivia and her unborn baby. Even now, she was a category all of her own. The precedence of the Myall Creek trials had people freaked out. Would some go to the gallows for this? Then what about the Captain? He had confessed without apology to defending the camp. Was self-defence a likely angle when he went there, intent on a fight? Henderson had returned and conducted a full review of McCray's managerial performance. The cattle had been found and accounted for. Duffing was no longer on the table as a charge. Henderson resumed running the station while McCray's case proceeded to the regional court. Ann's parents, Mr and Mrs Parsons, had come with money and an influential attorney named Jacobs, to see their grandson's father's name fully vindicated. Aunt Winifred had arrived with moral support and a lot of hats. Newspapers were rife with opinions and controversy. The scandalous kidnapping of Alex added a dimension to the sensationalism. To take an innocent child from his family was a step too far.

"Please state your name."

"Thelma Thane."

"What is your position at Henderson's Gap?"

"I am the nursery Nanny to Captain McCray's son, Alexander."

"How long have you been in this role?"

"Since he was born. He's now six years old. I was his wife's personal attendant before she was married. Her name was Ann... Ann Parsons. She died tragically when Alex was eight months old. I have been his mo... Nanny ever since."

"So, you are a trusted member of the family. You live with the family. And you were there when the events of May sixteenth unfolded. You can speak as a witness?"

"Yes."

"What is your recollection of the lead up to this day? What was the feel of the homestead?" There was an objection: relevance? Jacobs' short reply was "Goes to motive of the accused Your Honour."

"I remember tension. Everyone was on tenterhooks. The Captain was distressed because the schoolteacher was not working out. They had brought investigators from the Board of General Education to review her."

Jacobs looked down at his notes. "Your Honour; the following letters from the Board of General Education have been submitted as evidence. There exists a discrepancy between the correspondences. The first letter dated the eighth of March notifies of the complaint that had been submitted. This letter dated the fourteenth of April states the criteria had been satisfactorily met by the Henderson Gap School in all respects. These letters dated the twenty-first and thirtieth April respectively demand further evidence. If you look at the signatures, compared with this sample, it is my contention that these last two letters are fraudulent. Do you have an explanation, Miss Thane?"

"Me? What would I know? I am the Nanny."

"Your Honour, I submit blank stationery found in Miss Thanes personal effects. They have the seal of the Board of General Education. Do you wish to explain that Miss Thane?"

"Ridiculous! That is not mine. It can't be."

"I didn't assert they were yours, only that you had access to them, and they were found in your effects. Did you write those letters? You are under oath Miss Thane."

"I am not responsible for the tension caused by the gross inadequacies of the schoolteacher."

"Tension? You know the reasons for this feeling of unease?"

"When I think about it... really the whole feel of the station changed with the arrival of the teacher. Before that, there were no racial problems. Before that, there were no troubles in the household. Suddenly it all changed. He engaged her as a private governess. The Captain had to severely reprimand her for recklessly endangering Alexander's life. She took him down to the river; the boy's mother had drowned in a river! *And* they were always yelling. The Captain never raised his voice with his wife. He sacked her over that river incident. She was not suitable. He did the right thing."

"Yet Miss Wick was appointed as the provisional schoolteacher at Henderson's Gap School."

"I was surprised that he allowed *her* to teach the school. But I supposed it was just half-casts and station hand's kids... not children of position like his son. Yes, there was a lot of tension."

"You're suggesting the Captain, as you call Mister McCray, had no genuine regard for the Aborigines on the station under his guardianship?"

"No, no I am not suggesting that at all. The Captain is a benevolent man. He had oversight of the school. He was always down there trying to sort it out. But she is a power-hungry, manipulative and unprincipled woman. She was making a play for the Captain. He was out of her league, but she was determined. In the end, they were… ah… seeing each other. It is not surprising her engagement to Mister Hastings never worked out as she anticipated."

"You refer to Mister Leon Hastings of Fairfield Estate? And you know for certain she had been betrothed to Mister Hastings?"

"She had already lost him. Not surprising – he was a man of position in town. Mister Hastings came to the station. I met him. We talked. He was quite devastated. I comforted him."

Jacobs allow the irony to sit for a moment. "Mister Hastings was devastated… because he missed being with a wanton, unprincipled and manipulative woman. I would have thought that to be a relief. Is the man in his right mind?" The courtroom erupted. The presiding judge banged the gavel and demanded order.

A flush ran up her neck. "Of course, he was not devastated. We talked, that is all."

"He was devastated. He was not devastated. What was Hastings doing at Henderson's Gap that required your comfort?"

"Nothing happened! He confided in me, that is all."

"You said you comforted him. He confided his distress was because he wanted Miss Wick, the schoolteacher... to come back to Fairfield Estate?"

She looked uncertain. "Yes..."

"And you comforted him... in his grief?"

"Yes."

Jacobs considered his notes and then looked thoughtfully into the atmosphere. "So, here is one woman, a schoolteacher... no one of note, no family to speak of – with two very eligible suitors: Mister Hastings of Fairfield Estate; and Mister McCray, a former Captain in the Queen's army. And you... Miss Thane, you who comes from a respectable family, who has faithfully served this family... who cared and loved McCray's son as your own... and yet you, you do not have anyone."

"I did though! After Ann had died, I was to... I comforted him. He was to ..."

"The Captain, Mister McCray?"

"Yes."

"You seem to be a very comforting woman Miss Thane: Mister Hastings; Mister McCray..."

She sat starchily in her grey pinafore and glowered under her dark brows, as murmurings rippled over the gallery. She did not like the turn of the questioning. She could not resist the clarification that statement demanded. "My family in England has property! The Captain said I was a valued part of the family. He cared for me! Things *had* to go back to the way they were."

Jacobs abandoned his notes and continued. "You wanted things to go back to the way they were before Miss Wick arrived at the station… because Captain McCray cared for *you*?"

"Yes! And I cared for him too and…"

"Miss Thane. It would be more accurate to say you loved Captain McCray, and you took his regard for you as his son's nursery maid as evidence that he returned your affections."

"I thought if I was pregnant it would be proof. But afterwards the Captain said it was not going to happen again; that he had made a mistake. I hoped… but I wasn't. I am *not* a mistake! I had to prove I was pregnant, so I tried other ways…"

"How many 'other ways' are there to get pregnant Miss Thane?"

"There were stable-hands." She didn't even blush.

"So, you slept with the stable-hand to prove that the Captain loved *you*?"

"But it never meant anything. I just needed to be pregnant! Then it was too long. He would have known it was not his. By the time we came to Henderson's Gap, I was invisible…"

"It sounds like you have been misused and treated poorly Miss Thane. I imagine getting Miss Wick to leave Henderson's Gap was important."

"Hastings said if I could get the Wick girl to leave and go back to the city, he would pay me... handsomely. I said I could do that. I used that money and savings from my Christmas bonuses and hired the investigators. I organised the letters from the Board of General Education. Just because I am a Nanny doesn't mean I don't have feelings or brains. I went to a private school in England. I can do things. But he never even considered me to be Alexander's governess. This orphaned nobody was raised by a Chinese cook and a farmhand! She comes in and takes my life, my Captain, my Alexander. This should be my happy ending. She has no right. But she wouldn't leave! They weren't supposed to fight. She was just supposed to go."

"Tell me... I am fascinated, Miss Thane. It takes a great deal of cleverness to get an honoured military man to fight for something he just feels *benevolent* about. That doesn't sound particularly passionate. What would you have, that would give you that sort of leverage?"

"The Captain would do anything for his son. He left the army for him. He went from the military rank of Captain to a grazier out beyond nowhere. He did that for his son."

"From the prestige of a Ranking Officer... to a *farmer*?" His tone was disparaging.

"He was better than that. He was better than her. The kidnapping was not a real kidnapping. It was like you said: just leverage. It was all under control until that stock-hand got in the way. Jones took him. He said Alexander was safer with his wife's family. Family? They are savages! He said I was sick, but *he's* the one who was married to a savage. Jones said the boy was not safe with me and I should be locked up. But I protected him. I did. I always protect Alexander. I warned him I would shoot if he took the boy. And I did. I saved Alexander from the *real* kidnapping!"

"You shot Marshall Jones, the overseer at Henderson's Gap, for rescuing Alexander McCray from his kidnappers? These were the injuries he died from."

"No! No! That is not my fault. I saved Alex. I am the heroine here! I already said it was staged. It was not a real kidnapping."

"The child's family were threatened with the child's harm; there were demands that included a ransom of £5000. That *is* kidnapping Miss Thane."

"No! That was just to make it look authentic. Jones was the kidnapper! He took him away from me. I was just protecting Alexander until enough people could arrive from town to get him back." She paused with a sigh of relief. "The boy is safe now. He is okay. Life can go back to normal now. The rest is history."

Jacobs took off his eyeglasses and placed them on the desk in front of him. "That history, Miss Thane, is fifteen deaths. I fear life will never go back to normal for them, or their families. Nor you. How loved do you feel now?"

25.

Duncan stepped out into the light and tilted his face to the sun, his beard thick and matted from his months in the penitentiary. He breathed deeply of air that was not stale and he gathered Maggie into his arms.

He looked down into her eyes and realised that to be vindicated by one jury and condemned by another would be worse than the gallows. "A lifetime ago I asked a question and you told me that a jury would eventually deliver their verdict. What does the jury of Maggie's court determine?"

"You told me to learn your character. I have seen that... now..." She swallowed hard; her voice crackled with emotion. "When I went to the camp that day – all that violence and death... I didn't know how to picture you as a Captain of soldiers. No one talks about war like that. When I read stories of war I know it means fighting and blood and people dying, but I never actually thought about what that would be like. I never thought it would be as real as what I saw at the camp."

"I hated that you saw it. I wanted to spare you, and if I couldn't spare you, I wanted to erase the images. I haven't been able to do either."

"War really happens – it is not just a story. The times you were in the army... I could never see you in that place. I only wanted to see you at Henderson's Gap, sitting behind your desk in the library, or riding your horse."

"Does the jury have a verdict then, when the evidence is so ugly?"

"I have found that you are not Theseus, a slayer of monsters."

"What then?"

"I think you are more like Mordecai in the Bible – a defender of the people. I read the story of Queen Esther over and over. Mordecai was falsely accused because he would not bow down. He chose instead to empower powerless people, so the Hebrews could fight for their lives against annihilation on that day at Purim. That is what you did, Duncan. You are a Mordecai, a man of integrity: someone who would choose to stand up against the tide, and fight for those who cannot fight for themselves. And I am so grateful to be here with you now." She pressed herself against him not caring that his clothes were crushed and stale. She hardly dared to believe it was over.

"Thank you," he quietly whispered.

"I have prayed and prayed this day would come, that God would vindicate you. God has seen and honoured what you did."

He looked into her eyes. "And so, I found an ally in the White Queen: for 'such a time as this'." The relief that he felt swelled into a quiet elation. "So, you *are* Esther, my Queen, my White Queen," he said. She pulled back just slightly. Duncan looked at her hesitate. "When I was sitting in that cave, unable to move, it felt like checkmate. I was losing again," he said. "Yet something quite profound occurred to me. That one thought kept me through this whole ordeal. The thought was: *Maggie always plays white.*"

"Yes. I play white..." The picture played in her mind of them sitting across the table that first night... wearing her simple white frock and him in his casual dark house-clothes. The significance of that snippet of trivia eluded her. It seemed trite to reminisce their Wednesday night chess games just now after all they had been through. That was a lifetime ago.

"You see – that changed everything for me. I was looking at the Black King in checkmate – and it was true – he had no moves. But I remembered the Scripture says '*a man shall leave his father and his mother, and shall cleave unto his wife...*' That means it is my spiritual mandate for *me* to cleave to my wife... the one who plays white. I was looking at the wrong side. If the Black is in Checkmate, it means White is winning. I had to learn to play white; see everything from the other side. It gave me a different perspective. My head cleared. Internally I was free to move."

Maggie reached out and touched his face, tracing lines that were weary and strained. Her fingers stroked his beard, scruffy and rough. She was trying to understand what he was saying.

"Maggie I was so determined to ask you to be *my* Queen, but that is the wrong question. What I need to ask is if you will allow me to be *your* King? The White King."

She stared at him in the brightness of the street. Could he really be saying, after all he had been through, under all the constraints of prison, he held no resentment or disgust at the injustice of his trial? Was he free of all of that? If any doubt remained that she truly loved this man, it completely evaporated in that moment. He looked at her expectantly. "I'm asking you that question now. Maggie Wick, would you allow me to stand by your side? You have stood beside me during this ungodly trial. Will you to allow me to love and work and fight for you? Will you allow me to be your White King?"

She tilted her head as if she wasn't really catching what he was saying.

"Please. I want to be your White King!" He sounded almost desperate that she share his remarkable epiphany.

Maggie leaned forward and kissed him, tears filling her eyes. "Yes," she whispered, "Yes! Be my King. And I will be your Queen."

"Thank you, Maggie. Thank you," and he grimaced through what looked like physical pain as he took her in his arms. "White Queen – White King."

She lingered in the delight of his kiss, and gently pulled back with a smile, as she wiped her eyes. "You do remember the Queen is the most powerful piece on the board?"

"Oh yes. I am convinced this particular Queen hasn't a clue of the power she holds. But the game is won or lost on the position of the King. So, my royal one, we need each other." He caressed her hair and delighted in her smile. "So, tell me Maggie, has the Minotaur you feared so much, has he been slain?" he asked.

"Well, I know that Theseus has navigated the maze on his quest to kill the monster. I know that Theseus took a ball of red thread so that he could return victorious from the depths of that Cretan prison because here you are standing before me. But I wonder if the Minotaur – that vicious beast called Romance; I wonder if it has not been slain at all... but rather it has been tamed? I suspect that life does not go on without the Minotaur. I don't think I want it to. I think instead that the ending of the story is not what the mythological traditions determine, but rather that Theseus has tamed the wild beast and made it serve him. Perhaps the ending of the story is that Minotaur is not the enemy but an ally."

"Oh. So, my pretty Maggie Wick, do you think you could live with a monster called Romance... and allow it to become your servant? A servant that would dance, and play chess, and row boats with you?"

"I think I could live with such a beast. I think I would be heart-broken if the Romance Minotaur died."

"Then my mission as Theseus has changed: from being the slayer of such a beast... to being the Guardian of it." And he kissed her again, as a man who had been given back his life and saw that the value of the quest was not just in the victory, but in the struggle, and in the strategy, in the playing, and in the dance, held together by the red thread of grace, a thread that reunited and bound them together.

Epilogue

Tom jumped down from the saddle and pulled open the door of the stable, as Maggie followed and led her horse through. He hesitated, unsure of himself. "I didn't believe him," he said suddenly turning towards her.

"Didn't believe who?" she asked, as she unbuckled the girth.

"Him, whose name cannot be mentioned..."

"Oh. Tom, you do know that he is alive. He just lives in a different place now. So, we can talk about him… and mention his name – when we are together - if that is what you want."

He nodded. And swallowed. Tears welled behind his eyes.

"Tom, what did you find hard to believe?"

"Dad… he said you were a ripper on a horse. I never believed him." To a boy's heart, smashed and numb, it was glaringly disloyal.

Maggie pulled off the saddle and touched his shoulder. "Jones taught me to ride. He would never say a thing like that unless he meant it."

"But what if I had believed him? If I had, he might not have died. I should have believed him more."

Maggie sat down on some stooks of hay and quietly nudged him down beside her. "You did help that day, more than some grown men. You did everything your Dad asked of you. You took supplies to those who needed it. You saved lives. Nothing that happened that day was your fault, Tom. And you being there, right at the end... that was so brave. Your Dad was so sad to leave you but glad to be with Jesus at the same time. He lives there now. If there was any way he could have stayed here, he would have. I know that."

"But what if I can't... what if I can't forgive in here like he said?"

"It's hard to understand. Forgiving is not being happy about what happened. It's not even being okay with it. I'm not okay about any of what happened. I feel so sad and angry and hurt whenever I think about it. It was wrong from beginning to end." How could she explain something she was not completely sure about herself? "Forgiving is not easy to understand. But this is how I figure it: I can be angry about the wrong, and at the same time not demand revenge or payback, or want to make them suffer. By not taking that way, I forgive."

"They just get away with it?"

Maggie looked at his intense brown eyes and struggled with this herself, all over again. "We have our laws and it is right to apply them, although some of them don't seem to work too well. So, we do what we can. Thelma has been punished, but some of the other men weren't. People were enraged that Alex was kidnapped, but there are Takings from camps all the time and people say that is the right thing to do. More than once I thought the Captain would be penalised when he should have been considered a hero. There are lots of things that don't add up. But I have to believe, in the end, that justice is from God. I think that is what your Dad was meaning. We pray against the fear, pray for peace, and courage to keep on doing the next thing that works towards making things better. You taught me that, remember? Courage to do the next thing, which for you, straight after lunch, will be maths problems."

Tom groaned. He hadn't learnt to like Maths any better. They had morning chores to do and then classes started in the afternoon, in the nursery. Priscilla's morning was learning to be a governess with Maggie; Jemima liked cooking and was getting lessons from Lonnie; Tom went about the station with Duncan or Blondie, who was now Head Stockman; Andy and Keziah helped Sammy in the garden. The younger ones, Alex and Keren, did odd jobs like feeding the chooks or raking the paths before they could play. Terry the Cockatoo supervised them with his permanently singed tail and cocky attitude. It was to be this way until a schoolteacher could be reinstated. Even now, some parents were starting to realise what had been lost and were talking with the Captain about building a new schoolhouse.

"Tom, you know your Dad meant it when he said he was really proud of you?" She was silent for a moment, reverently holding the memory. "Come, we had better do the next thing now and get ready for lunch, or Lonnie will be after us."

They gathered around the long table in the dining room and Duncan said grace. Lunch was a noisy, energetic affair. Lonnie handed out slices of fresh bread and fillings for sandwiches. Tom passed the plum-and-melon jam on quickly. He just couldn't get over the idea that he had been hoodwinked into taking something that had drugged him to sleep. Even little Alex made jokes about Lonnie's jam after he had been told he slept through an entire afternoon and night when they had to go into the bush to practise shadowing. He remembers Tom handing him his bear as his Dad took him in his arms and carried him back to his bed; and then sharing his room with the whole Jones' clan, like another campout. That was the start of their new family.

Duncan tapped his glass with his fork and cleared his throat as he gazed proudly across at his wife. "I have two important family announcements to make. The first is important for our family. You know that Mister Henderson was here while I was away for Court, and he has been back a number of times. We have spoken a lot lately, because with Misses Henderson's health the way it is, he is no longer able to keep the station. Today I got a letter to say he has accepted our offer. With some help from family, we are going to buy Henderson's Gap. So, we can stay. This is our home!" A cheer erupted from around the table, and Duncan waited for the commotion to settle.

"My next announcement is…" he paused for dramatic effect, "very important too. Maggie is expecting a baby and we need to give her all the care and attention we can." Maggie glowed. Celebrations and laughter. And then she grinned a little broader as she realised Duncan had no idea she was still riding horses. Perhaps this baby would be the daughter they had joked about so long ago, a lifetime ago.

The ruckus settled and little mouths began to fill with lunch, Maggie smiled as a pair of common peewees chimed out an endorsement, their triplet notes singing a rhythmic duet. Those birds are very loyal, fiercely territorial and in their ordinary way, uniquely special. She was learning to sing peewee. Maggie, the White Queen with her White King, had found the music of home.

&⚬&

About the Author

 Born in the wrong century, Olwyn Harris has spent a lot of time craving time-travel in a way that can include life essentials like Belgium milk chocolate, air-conditioning and laptops. With a passion for companioning people in their stories, whether they be real or trumped-up, she takes inexplicable pleasure in finding the common ground in our human and spiritual experiences. She is enamoured with the mystery of how the ordinary transforms to extraordinary when given a generous brush-down with the presence of prayer and considers it her personal life-quest to find the heroine in all of us.

When she is not time-travelling, she lives in the Whitsundays; is a wife, mother, counsellor, pastor, and spiritual director.

By The Same Author

Matt's Boys of Wattle Creek

 When Matthew Lawson's three sons were born, he wrote each of them a letter outlining his hopes and prayers for their futures. When he decided to give up his city job and move to the little town of Wattle Creek, he could never have imagined the effect it would have on his young family. As Matt's boys grow into maturity and find their places in their community, will his dreams and prayers come to fulfilment? Will his boys develop their own faith in the eternal God? And will they each find the kind of love that Matt holds for his beautiful Josie?